CHAPTER 1

"*B*eware…" the ghostly voice said. "Beware…"

The ghost's torn robe fluttered in the chilly wind, the rags whipping around his knees. Old Mayor Townsend's bronze face was a sickly green. His eyes sparkled red as they gazed over Alice's head at Blithedale's Main Street.

"Too creepy?" Ona asked, popping out from behind the statue where she'd been hiding and pretending to be the old mayor's ghost.

"Is that one of the inn's bathrobes?"

"Yup. Torn to shreds."

"And the rhinestone eyes and the green face—well done."

"But temporary. If it rains, the green paint will run. I'll have to remember to reapply. So, what do you think?"

"Hmm…he still looks too—" Alice cocked her head. "—serious."

Ona stood next to Alice, regarding the statue. Then stepped up to the old mayor, dug into her pocket, and brought out a lipstick. She applied some to his face and stepped away.

"There. That's better."

"Much better." Alice smiled. "Now he looks friendly."

The statue of Old Mayor Townsend, decked out in a ghostly costume, now had a big red smile on his face. It made him look goofy and harmless, which was how Alice liked her Halloween.

Inside the Pemberley Inn, the phone rang and Ona rushed inside. Alice put another carved pumpkin with a light on the inn's porch. Ona's voice murmured through the front doors.

The wind gusted through Blithedale, and leaves of many colors tumbled down Main Street. Alice hugged herself. Next week, it would be Halloween, and each day it seemed to get a little colder.

She stepped inside the old Victorian mansion, shutting the door behind her. On a chilly day like this, entering the lobby of the Pemberley Inn, with its thick oriental rugs and cozy decor, felt like slipping into a favorite wool sweater.

Still on the phone, Ona said, "That's confirmed then—we look forward to seeing you on Friday." She hung up and beamed. "Eight guests. Eight! That means every single room at the inn is booked for Halloween weekend."

As she smiled, the red rhinestones on her eye-patch glittered. Alice couldn't help but smile, too. Ona's happiness was infectious. Yet a small, familiar voice in her mind scolded her for taking advantage of her friend. After all the time she'd spent in Blithedale, Alice still lived in the Colonel Brandon Suite upstairs, free of charge. But, as Ona had pointed out, Alice couldn't afford to pay and Ona couldn't afford to have her best friend move out of her house, so the arrangement was a win-win.

More of a win for you, the voice told her.

Alice ignored the old, critical voice. It might stay with her for many years to come, but she'd learned to listen to more sensible voices. Like Ona's.

A HALLOWEEN TO DIE FOR

A WONDERLAND BOOKS COZY MYSTERY

BOOK THREE

M.P. BLACK

For A.

Ona said, "Word is spreading about Blithedale. It's a long drive from the city, but people will gladly come for the fall leaves."

"And the pumpkins."

"Yes, and don't forget the haunted house."

Alice had seen the advertisements, of course. In fact, Ona had pegged one to the side of the reception desk:

Dr. Fantasma's Thrilling Adventures Presents:
The Blithedale Haunted House Experience.

The illustration showed an old ramshackle Victorian mansion tangled in cobwebs, with a skeleton sitting in a rocker on the front porch. Alice leaned closer. She'd looked at the poster several times before, yet there was a detail she'd never noticed before. Someone was peeking around a curtain at an attic window. The shrunken face of a ghoul, its eyes burning with malice.

The door to the inn banged open, and Alice's heart clenched. She spun around.

A man came through the entrance, pulling a small suitcase. He shut the door behind him with another bang.

He wore a dark suit, white shirt, no tie, and over that, a blue wool trench coat. His salt-and-pepper hair was perfectly coiffed, and when he smiled, he revealed teeth that would've made an orthodontist proud. He wasn't shy about showing them, either.

Alice, who'd pressed a hand to her chest, said, "You startled me."

"I should be the one to be startled." He looked from Ona to Alice, and then back to Ona again. "Blithedale is known for its natural beauty, but I see it's an understatement."

Alice glanced over at Ona. She pressed her lips tight. She was suppressing an emotion. Judging by the twinkle in her one visible eye, it was hilarity. The man's sweet talking didn't impress Alice, either, but she was more inclined to a grimace than a smile.

Ona consulted her computer.

"Welcome back, Mr. Conway."

"Stewart."

"I've got your room ready."

"I booked a suite."

"Are you expecting someone will join you?"

"You never know." That big smile flashed again as he stared at Ona. "You never know."

Ona ignored him. Alice leaned against the bottom banister of the staircase, watching the interaction. She'd met men like Stewart Conway before: wealthy, confident, and convinced of their own magnificence. She detested the type, but some women—incomprehensibly—absolutely loved guys like that.

Ona was detailing the many things to do in Blithedale on his visit.

"There's also a haunted house event," she concluded, gesturing toward the poster on the front of the reception.

"I know," he said. "It's my property."

"You're not Dr. Fantasma, are you?" Alice asked.

Stewart Conway looked over his shoulder at her and chuckled. "God, no. I own the properties Dr. Fantasma and his crew use for their so-called thrilling adventures. In fact, I own two dozen haunted houses across five states."

He looked around, studying the Pemberley's decor. A series of portraits graced the staircase wall, each one depicting a character from Jane Austen's novels. In the reception, there was a large framed oil painting of the fictional Pemberley—Darcy's estate in *Pride & Prejudice*—which bore little resemblance to Ona's Victorian mansion.

"I've always thought this inn was nice. I bet you do a good business."

"I do fine," Ona said modestly.

"How'd you like to expand? I've got a property that might interest you." He leaned against the reception counter, dropping his voice to a low, suggestive murmur. "I'd offer an excellent price—" He paused. Smiled. "—for a friend."

Ona grabbed the key to the room. "You've got lucky friends, Mr. Conway."

"Call me Stewart, please."

"Right this way, Mr. Conway."

Alice marveled at Ona's ability to be firm while still sounding friendly. She pushed back on Stewart Conway's come-on without giving him any cause for offense. Obviously, she'd dealt with the Conways of the world before—maybe even this Conway. Now she gestured for her guest to go ahead of her to one of the rooms on the first floor.

"Please, ladies first," he said.

Ona ignored it with a friendly smile. Finally, he gave a shrug and headed down the hallway, rolling the suitcase behind him.

There had been a moment there when Alice had wondered, worried, whether Stewart Conway was one of those men who got angry at rejection.

As Ona passed her, Alice whispered, "Want me to come?"

"He's harmless," Ona muttered, "unless you invite him into your room."

That sounded ominously as if Stewart Conway were a vampire. Alice watched Ona escort Conway down the corridor toward his suite. Well, if anyone could handle a bloodsucker, it was Ona.

After they'd vanished from sight, Alice continued to add Halloween decorations to the reception. She'd closed her bookstore, Wonderland Books, only an hour before, and darkness was falling outside. Once this job was done and things calmed down for Ona, they'd head over to the What the Dickens Diner for dinner.

Ona returned to the reception alone. When Alice asked her how it went with Mr. Conway, she rolled her eye. "The guy's got no shortage of self-confidence."

Ona expected no more guests that day. She had to prepare a room for an arrival in the morning, though. Alice helped her gather fresh linens, towels, and a bathrobe, and while Ona made the bed, Alice headed to the pantry off the kitchen to fetch a basket of complimentary goodies. This one had a Halloween twist: a tourist map of Blithedale, a small bag of candy, and a flyer advertising Dr. Fantasma's haunted house.

Alice was crossing the hallway to return to the room Ona was making up when she spotted Stewart Conway through the glass in the front door. Apparently, he was on his way out, but he'd stopped on the steps to talk to another man. Or that man had stopped him. They seemed to be having an argument.

Alice, pretending to need something from the reception, positioned herself by Ona's computer. She glanced over.

The men didn't seem to have noticed her. Stewart Conway had his back toward her, and the other man was too busy jabbing a finger in Conway's face. Conway's companion was a thickset man with the arms of a weight-lifter and a grim scar down one cheek. He jabbed the finger at Conway again, and even through the doors, she could hear his angry voice.

"You have no idea of the damage…"

Conway said something, maintaining a calm tone of voice. As a result, Alice couldn't make out the words.

"You bastard," the other man snarled. "You think because you own the property, you can do what you want."

Conway laughed and spoke again, once more too faintly for Alice to hear.

The other man clenched his fists and drew one arm back. For a moment, Alice was sure he was going to leap at Conway and punch him. But instead, he clenched his jaw and took a step away from him. He loosened his hands.

"We're talking about people's lives here," he said. Then he ran a finger across his throat in a threatening gesture. "Your own, too."

A chill went down Alice's spine as she watched the man walk away.

CHAPTER 2

*O*ver the next couple of days, Alice couldn't shake a feeling of unease. She enjoyed the festive preparations for Halloween, decorating the bookstore, drinking hot apple cider, and soaking up the riotous colors of the Blithedale Woods. But underneath it all ran a low thrum of dread. Something didn't feel right. And it was more than just the spooky season getting under her skin. Something about the threat she'd overheard…

On Tuesday, she was restocking her shelves with a shipment of books she'd eagerly anticipated for her Halloween display. The boxes contained classics like *Frankenstein* by Mary Shelley, *Dracula* by Bram Stoker, and *The Turn of the Screw* by Henry James. Plus, more recent ones by Stephen King, Grady Hendrix, Tiffany D. Jackson, Victoria Schwab, and Ryan Douglass. She made a display for kids with *Room on the Broom*, *Creepy Pair of Underwear!*, and *That Monster on the Block*, and half a dozen other kid-friendly Halloween books.

She was reaching up to the top of one of her bookshelves, slipping a book into place, when she sensed someone stood behind her. But when she turned toward the entrance, expecting to see a customer, the shop was empty. The wind blew through the open door. The draft prickled her arms and left goosebumps in its wake.

Alice stood still. When nothing happened, she stepped down from her stool. On her way down, she knocked a book off the bookshelf, and it fell to the floor with a smack.

She crouched down and picked it up.

It was a used book donated by someone in Blithedale. Her stock was a mix of used and new books. When she'd opened her bookstore, Alice's budget had been tight. Eager to help, people all over town brought her boxes and boxes of old hardbacks and paperbacks. Sometimes she discovered real treasures.

This was a copy of Lewis Carroll's poem, "Jabberwocky," with intricate illustrations. She remembered the book from her childhood. It had fascinated and frightened her in equal measure when her mom read it to her.

She opened the book. On the inside page, a handwritten note said,

From Mom to Alice – such a Merry Christmas and so much love.

Alice's breath caught in her throat. She looked up, certain that she would see someone standing in her store.

But no one was there.

"Mom?" she whispered.

The wind gusted through the open door, and a single red leaf tumbled across the floor. Clutching the book to her chest, Alice went to the front door and looked out. Blithedale's Main Street looked no different than usual. Well, apart from the many pumpkins, fake cobwebs, and ghosts fluttering from lamp posts.

She checked her phone. It was time to close the bookstore. She shut the red door and turned around, and another wave of goosebumps spread across her arms.

She was sure she would turn and see someone standing there.

But her bookstore was empty. Of course, it was.

She shook her head. How many used books did locals bring in every week? Countless. And how many of her own books—remnants from her childhood—must be circulating among locals? Discovering a book that had once been a gift from her mom was a strange occurrence. But strange occurrences weren't the same as paranormal phenomena.

There's no such thing as ghosts, she told herself.

But that didn't mean that she didn't feel her mom's presence. Ever since she'd come back to Blithedale, and especially since opening her own bookstore, she'd sensed her mom. She wasn't like a ghost, though. She was more of a feeling—a feeling of no longer being so alone.

When Alice was nine, her mom got cancer. She sold the bookstore in Blithedale, and they moved away so her mom could get treatment. She'd died within months. From the age of nine, Alice had lived with her aunt and uncle and learned to be self-reliant, convinced that life was a series of struggles done alone. Looking back now, Alice felt sad for her younger self—a little girl who had suffered from such intense loneliness. A little girl who grew into a lonely adult.

But then, on the verge of getting married to a man she didn't love, she'd run from her own wedding. She'd fled back to Blithedale, and discovered a town full of happy memories —and the promise of a new beginning.

A crazy idea occurred to her. What if a spirit had lived in her mom's bookstore, and it was this ghost that had led Alice back to Blithedale?

"Thank you," she whispered to the empty bookstore,

feeling a little ridiculous. But maybe also a little hopeful. What if a ghost really was here? If it had led her to this new life, she was grateful.

She had much to be thankful for. Opening Wonderland Books had only been possible with the support of the community. Specifically, her friends Becca and Ona, who'd set up the Blithedale Future Fund to provide loans for businesses like hers.

Ona had even built the bookstore. It was a tiny house, a miniature log cabin crammed with books and measuring only about 400 square feet. Its interior contained leftover materials from her mom's bookstore, and the red front door would forever remind Alice of the "hideaway" she'd retreated to in that old shop. She didn't think her mom remained as a ghost. But maybe something—or someone—else from her mom's store had remained in Wonderland's walls…

"Thank you," she said, louder this time, looking around for some sign of an answer, her stomach in a knot. What might happen? Lights flickering. Another book falling from the shelves. Or something dangerous?

What if the ghost was evil?

She shuddered, looking around her store, suddenly seeing too many deep shadows in the nooks and crannies of Wonderland.

Then stopped herself. What she was seeing was her cozy bookstore, nothing else.

Ghosts? Please.

Why was she getting so worked up? Even if she believed in ghosts—and she wasn't so sure of that—she certainly wasn't afraid of them. After all, she'd faced flesh-and-blood murderers. Why be spooked by something as harmless as a bookstore spirit?

She put her hands on her hips and addressed the "ghost."

"I'm about to close," she said. "So you're going to have to

leave soon."

As if in answer to her statement, the door to the bookstore flew open. The wind whirled dead leaves inside, and Alice's heart leaped into her throat and huddled there, like a frightened animal.

"Alice…"

Alice whipped around, ready to face whatever ghost or ghoul had flown in.

But it was a living person standing in the doorway, holding a pile of boxes. Ona peered around her heavy load.

"Wanna give me a hand with these?"

Alice's heart slinked back down to her chest, where it belonged, and she laughed at herself as she took the top box from Ona. She closed the door behind her.

"What's so funny?" Ona asked.

"I thought you were a ghost."

"Getting into the Halloween spirit, huh?"

"Yeah, maybe a little too much."

They put the boxes on the counter. Inside were more used books, and judging by the top ones, they were in good condition.

"Who donated these?" Alice asked.

"I found them outside the bookstore just now. No note on them." Alice got busy digging into the boxes, pulling out the most interesting books.

Ona grabbed her arm and pulled her away. "That, my dear, can wait." She grinned. "Dr. Fantasma and his crew have arrived—they're hanging out at the diner. I say we go see what they're all about and grab a bite."

Agreeing to her Ona's proposal, Alice turned off the lights, but before locking the front door, she took a last look at her bookstore, now dark.

"Goodnight," she whispered.

Then closed the door.

CHAPTER 3

*A*t Becca's restaurant, the What the Dickens Diner, the decor was usually dominated by framed illustrations from Charles Dickens novels. The prints were still hanging on the walls, but now fake cobwebs covered them, rubber spiders clung to the frames, and by a booth near the back, a human-sized skeleton hovered on wires overhead. They contrasted with the classic formica tabletops and red leatherette seats in the booths.

The air in the diner smelled of Becca's pumpkin muffins and hot apple cider. Music played at a low volume. Alice recognized the Halloween classic, "Monster Mash." It conjured happy memories of trick-or-treating with her mom, carving pumpkins, and making Halloween costumes out of old clothes and cardboard, with a dash of glue and glitter. She also remembered watching *It's the Great Pumpkin, Charlie Brown* on TV, and that familiar jazzy shuffle of the Vince Guaraldi soundtrack.

Across the diner, Alice spotted Susan, the waitress, serving customers at the counter. Becca sat at a window table talking to someone. To Alice's surprise, it was Stewart Conway.

But before Alice could give it more thought, Ona interrupted her.

"Come on." She grabbed Alice's hand. "Let's go say hi to Dr. Fantasma."

"Is that really his name?"

"Oh, it's probably something like Harold Smith, but I bet he'd never tell you that. He's big on mysteries."

At the back of the diner, three strangers sat in a booth—two men and a woman.

Coming closer, Alice stifled a gasp.

"What?" Ona asked, looking back at her.

Alice had stopped. She recognized one of the people in the booth—the man who'd threatened Stewart Conway.

"Nothing. I'll tell you later."

Ona nodded and tugged her along.

"Dr. Fantasma," she said, addressing the older of the two men. "You remember me?"

"Of course I remember you, Ona. The only person I know who wears an eye patch that isn't part of a trick."

He said it with a warm smile and dramatic wave of the hand that made it sound complimentary. In another man's mouth, it might've caused offense. But Dr. Fantasma was all old-school charm. He must've been in his early seventies, with white hair slicked back from his tall forehead, bushy eyebrows, and a white mustache. The black cloak with purple velvet lining he wore made him look like a 1940s screen actor—someone like Boris Karloff.

"When will I convince you to come visit my inn, Dr. Fantasma?" Ona asked.

"But where would we park our caravansary? We are well provided for at the illustrious Blithedale Campgrounds."

Alice glanced at the other two people at the table. A

mousy-haired woman with tired eyes. And the man who'd threatened Mr. Conway—a hard, watchful look on his face, as if he were a predator ready to strike.

"But tell me, Ona, who is your friend here?"

Ona pulled Alice forward. "This is Alice Hartford."

"Hartford, Hartford…" Dr. Fantasma said, furrowing his brows, as if trying to remember something. Then snapped his fingers. "I once knew a Hartford. She owned a bookstore in Blithedale."

"That was my mom," Alice said.

"She solved a rather vexing mystery for me. See, I had a rare coin. An antique. Of inestimable value."

He reached into his cloak, and holding out his hand, revealed a coin.

It was larger than any coin Alice had seen before, and it bore a strange symbol on its face, like a hieroglyph of an eye. An eyebrow slashed over the eye. A line extended curved from the corner of the eye, another straight down from the bottom.

Dr. Fantasma said, "The Eye of Horus. A powerful protection against evil. I never leave home without it. For anyone who transacts business with the hereafter must carry protection." He clenched his fist. Then leaned toward Alice. "So, imagine my horror when it went missing…"

He opened his hand. The coin had vanished.

"But thanks to your mother," he said, "it returned to me."

Alice said, "Where was it? Who took it?"

Dr. Fantasma chuckled. "Why you did, Alice. Check your pocket."

He gestured toward her and Alice, confused for a moment, realized he literally meant for her to reach into the pocket of her jeans. She did so—and found, to her astonishment, the missing coin. Then a memory niggled at the back of her mind. The memory of a tall man in a multicolored cloak making a coin disappear and then reappear in her own pocket. She couldn't have been more than 7 years old.

She handed the coin back to him. "How did you—?"

"Dr. Fantasma never reveals the mysteries of his magic." He smiled. "But please, promise me you will visit our haunted house experience."

"I don't know…"

In her opinion, haunted houses—and other Halloween entertainments—had become too inspired by slasher horror films in recent years. These days, the point seemed to traumatize people, not entertain them. What happened to the whimsy? What happened to the Charlie Brown version of the holiday?

Fortunately, most of Blithedale still subscribed to the old-fashioned, family-fun version of Halloween with carved pumpkins and Casper-like ghosts.

She knew Becca and Ona felt the same as her. But what about Dr. Fantasma's haunted house?

Ona said, "Don't worry, Alice. Dr. Fantasma's stuff is fun and violence free—not like those terrifying experiences that send people to the emergency room. It's old school."

"Thank you, Ona," Dr. Fantasma said with a smile. "In my book, *old school* is a compliment."

"Oh, it definitely is," Alice said. "Violence free sounds good."

Just then, a raised voice made Alice turn around. Across the diner, Becca had gotten to her feet. She brandished a steak knife in her hand, glaring down at Stewart Conway.

"You've got a lot of nerve," she said.

"Becca, my—"

"Don't you try to sweet talk me. Leave my diner right away, or I'll make you."

She pointed the knife at him.

Calmly, with an amused expression on his face, Stewart

Conway gathered up his stylish blue coat and got to his feet. He stared at Becca, clearly about to speak again.

"I'm not kidding," she said, taking a step closer.

She gripped the hilt of the knife so hard that her knuckles turned white. Alice noticed it, and so did Conway.

He dropped a bill on the table. Then said, "Happy to take my business down the street to the Darn Good Diner."

He swiveled around and strode out of the diner. Becca stood still for a moment, her hand still clenched around the steak knife as she glared at the door as it swung shut.

Then she looked around at the patrons. Except for the music, which blithely continued with Louis Armstrong's "The Skeleton in the Closet," the diner had gone dead quiet.

She looked down at the knife. Then slapped it down on the formica table, tore off her apron, and rushed out the back of the diner.

CHAPTER 4

*A*lice put an arm around Becca. From the back steps of the diner, they had a view of the parking lot. Trash cans stood lined up against the wall nearby. Where the parking lot ended, the Blithedale Woods began, the trees swaying in the wind.

Ona sat down on the other side of Becca and wrapped an arm around her, too.

"What happened in there?" Alice asked.

Becca drew in a long breath and let it out.

"Stewart Conway happened."

She looked down at her hands and shook her head.

"But that's not even the truth. Stewart is Stewart. Always has been and always will be. Full of himself. Manipulative. Years ago, at a time when I was lonely, I didn't see the big red flags. I didn't want to see them. So, I learned the hard way."

Becca paused. She looked across the parking lot at the dense woods, and Alice followed her gaze. Within the forest, it was already full dark. As the trees shook, leaves fell. The wind picked them up and sent them dancing across the parking lot.

As she so often did, Alice felt a sense of wonder at living in this little nook in the great woods. Life was good in Blithedale. Or at least it ought to be.

"Do you want to talk about it?" Alice asked.

"About Stewart? Not really. Besides, he's not the real reason I snapped in there. I'm stressed. I didn't think I was. I thought I could handle it. But there's no way around it…"

Alice glanced over at Ona, and Ona gave a shrug, showing she didn't know what Becca might stress about. Becca, who was a human rock, seemed to weather every storm with an incredible strength and stoicism. But no person was a rock, of course. Everyone had their Achilles heel. And Alice was pretty sure she knew which one was Becca's.

"Anything happening with the diner that's upsetting you?" she asked.

"That new place…"

"The Darn Good Diner," Ona said.

Alice knew the new diner by sight, though she hadn't visited it yet. She knew Ona hadn't either.

Becca nodded. "When the new diner opened last month, I thought, 'Great, another restaurant. Blithedale needs more restaurants. The more the merrier.' I still believe that. Only —" She sighed. "Only Gretchen Tusk—she's the owner— she's going out of her way to undermine my business. Instead of developing her own concept, she's copying mine and then slashing prices. At first, I thought, 'Fine, she'll never get far this way.' But she's continuing to keep prices low, and copying more and more of my menu and specials, and I can see the effect. I'm losing customers. This time of year should be extra busy. But seats are empty. I'm not selling enough."

"But Becca, it's not as if your own margins are big," Ona said. "As you pointed out, Gretchen can't keep doing this forever."

"Maybe not. But what if she can keep going for a year? Where will that leave me?"

Alice tightened her arm around Becca, and she felt Ona do the same.

Alice said, "We'll help. We're sticking with the What the Dickens Diner through thick and thin. Got it?"

"Got it," Becca said.

The talk lifted Becca's spirits. A minute later, she strode back inside her diner, put the apron back on, and got to work with her usual energy. Alice and Ona found seats at the counter, each ordering the meatloaf special with mashed potatoes and then watching Becca to make sure she was all right.

When they'd both finished, Ona said, "Are you thinking what I'm thinking?"

Alice nodded. "Let's go take a look at this new diner."

CHAPTER 5

he Darn Good Diner lay in a fork in the road at the far end of Main Street. Alice and Ona approached on foot, taking the reconnaissance as an opportunity for a brisk walk.

"Not as central a location as the What the Dickens Diner," Alice said.

"Yeah, but everyone passes this fork on their way in and out of town. You can't miss the diner. And look at that parking lot."

Ona was right. The gravel parking lot spilled onto a grassy field before hitting the ubiquitous forest. Unlike Becca's limited spaces, this lot could accommodate a heavy influx of guests—more than you'd ever be able to fit inside the diner.

Alice pulled open the door to the diner and followed Ona inside.

The Darn Good Diner had formica tables and plastic seats and none of the vintage charm of Becca's diner. Nor, of course, the quirky Charles Dickens theme.

But most people won't pay extra for a dash of Dickens.

What might attract them, however, were cozy Halloween decorations, and Gretchen Tusk had decked out her restaurant with pumpkins and cobwebs and plastic skeletons, similar to what Becca had done. In fact, precisely as Becca had done. There was even the skeleton hovering over a booth at the back.

"Looks familiar, doesn't it?" Ona said.

"Same kinds of decorations," Alice agreed. "But cheaper. Becca's brought out her old Halloween trinkets, some of them homemade. This stuff looks like it won't last through the season. Cute. But dollar-store cute."

"It's not hurting business, though."

Ona was right. The place was hopping, with every booth and table occupied and only a few empty stools at the counter. A woman with curly hair as red as paprika came toward them with a big smile on her face. Her diner uniform had a small name tag that said, "Gretchen."

"Can I get you two seated? I've got a couple of prime spots at the counter."

Ona glanced at Alice, who gave her friend a shrug as if to say, "Sure, let's do this…"

Gretchen led them to the counter and handed them a menu. The counter ran along the left-hand wall of the diner with the back opening onto its small kitchen. A young guy wearing a bandana stood back there, moving swiftly between flipping burgers, submerging fries in oil, and chopping fruit and vegetables.

Alice slipped onto the stool and began to read the menu as Ona joined her.

"Wow," Ona said. "Just wow."

Alice was at a loss for words. Becca hadn't been kidding. The menu looked identical to the one at the What the Dickens Diner. Leaving aside the absence of Dickensian references, the word choice was almost the same.

One thing was different, though.

"How is a burger with fries half the price of what it is at Becca's?" Alice asked.

"And Becca already charges next to nothing compared to the city," Ona said, shaking her head. "Look at the price of this meatloaf special. And the Cobb salad. And the pancakes…"

Gretchen appeared on the other side of the counter. "Sounds like you're finding a lot to like. What can I get you?"

Ona frowned, her one visible eye narrowing, and Alice put a cautioning hand on her leg. They knew little about Gretchen—maybe there was a good explanation for all this.

"Benefit of the doubt…" she muttered under her breath, so only Ona could hear.

Alice put down her menu and spoke to Gretchen. "Actually, we just ate at the What the Dickens. So maybe two decaf coffees?"

Gretchen's smile vanished. Her eyes narrowed. "Did that Becca Frye woman send you?"

"Nobody sent us. We—"

"You're her friends."

"Sure we are, but—"

She snatched the menus away from them and walked away, turning her back on them.

"Friendly, too," Ona said. "What were you saying about the benefit of the doubt?"

Alice didn't like it—the rock-bottom prices, the obvious copy-catting—and she didn't like Gretchen Tusk. Least of all did she like the fact that the diner was packed with both out-of-towners and locals. She could see why Becca was worried.

She looked around at the crowd, trying to find Stewart Conway, but he was nowhere in sight. Maybe his threat to go to the rival diner had been empty, after all.

Her eyes landed on a couple of familiar faces at the other end of the counter. A couple of familiar heads of hair, too.

Alice had met the two young women, Edie and Fleur, during an investigation into the death of the previous owner of the Blithedale Theater. Edie and Fleur both had the same tint of purple hair. They had come to Blithedale following a true crime podcaster, but they'd stayed, falling in love with the town.

Alice pointed them out to Ona.

"I don't think they've had any luck finding work," Ona said. "They're staying at the campgrounds and spend their days hanging out. I've seen them at Bonsai & Pie and at Becca's diner. But I never see them eating full meals, just ordering coffee and tap water."

Alice knew it wasn't easy to find work in a small town like Blithedale. She wished she could hire the two of them, but Wonderland Books, though it was doing well, wasn't bringing in enough money yet to justify getting an employee, let alone two.

The two men who sat next to Alice and Ona finished their meal and paid just as Gretchen brought coffees for them, serving them without looking at them. Alice used the opportunity to move over to the vacated seats and say hello to Edie and Fleur.

"Hi, Alice," Edie said, and looked down at her lap as if embarrassed. "Hi, Ona."

Fleur gave a little awkward wave.

"You girls still staying at the campgrounds?" Ona asked. "I've seen you hanging around town. At Bonsai & Pie. At Becca's diner. Why don't you come hang out at the Pemberley Inn? I've got a nice lounge you're welcome to use."

Edie looked at Fleur, who gave a noncommittal shrug.

"Super nice of you," Fleur mumbled. "Maybe we'll take you up on that sometime."

"Like *super* nice," Edie said, nodding.

Alice could relate to their obvious discomfort. She herself got uncomfortable when people offered to give her anything for free—she'd been raised by her aunt and uncle to view such things as charity. Self-reliance, which was what Alice had cultivated from the time her mom died, dictated that you do things on your own and you pay for yourself. After coming to Blithedale, though, she'd come to see things differently. Becca and Ona had showed her that there was more than one way to give, and that friendship and community depended on opening your arms to receive as much as it depended on reaching out to give.

She was trying to think of a way to encourage Edie and Fleur to accept Ona's offer—something that wouldn't sound condescending—when the door to the diner flew open and a voice called out: "Ladies and gentlemen!"

She turned. So did Ona, Edie, and Fleur.

Dr. Fantasma stood in the doorway, his arms raised as the hem of his cloak swayed around his legs. He strode inside.

"In two days, nay two nights," he said, speaking with an exaggerated, theatrical voice, "you will experience the greatest wonder of your lives. If—and only if—you choose to join me at my latest thrilling adventure, the Blithedale Haunted House."

Ona leaned close to Alice and whispered, "I swear, this guy must have stepped through a time portal—he's pure vaudeville."

Alice smiled. As Dr. Fantasma described the haunted house experience in colorful detail, peppering every sentence with antiquated adjectives, she watched the effect on the people in the diner. People smiled and looked at each other and then smiled some more. Parents leaned close to their kids and explained things, maybe mentioning how Dr. Fantasma had wowed them when they were kids.

He might be old school, but Dr. Fantasma knew how to entertain.

His companions—the young woman and the tough guy— hurried from table to table, handing out flyers advertising the haunted house. Meanwhile, Dr. Fantasma's sales pitch continued, his voice booming to the four corners of the diner, and soon he had people laughing and clapping.

But under the growing volume, Alice overheard voices struggling to remain low. The sounds came from the kitchen.

"Calm down," Gretchen hissed.

"The money, Gretchen," the young chef said.

"They didn't build Rome in one day."

"If you don't—"

"Shh…I'll make it right, Dylan. Don't worry. Another couple of days is all I need."

The guy—Dylan—turned away. With his back to her, he continued to chop vegetables. "You got two days. After that, I do this my way."

Gretchen looked up and, seeing Alice, frowned.

Alice got busy drinking her coffee, pretending not to eavesdrop.

CHAPTER 6

*T*hat night, the wind picked up, and the temperature dropped. The constant shushing of leaves played like white noise behind Blithedale's daily activities, and it put Alice on edge.

It shouldn't have. She loved the sound of leaves rustling, of trees shaking themselves with a swish and a sigh, as if nature were performing the last act of a stately ballet. She loved the seasons, all four acts. Yet she jumped at every sharp noise—a book dropped, a car door slammed, a child's playful scream.

The next night, asleep in her canopy bed in the Colonel Brandon Suite, she opened her eyes to darkness.

A sound had woken her.

Creaking floorboards.

The sound came from above—from the Pemberley Inn's attic.

Ghosts, she told herself, *only exist in books and movies.*

She turned over on her pillow, pressing it against her face. Eventually, after much tossing and turning, she fell back asleep.

The next day, she felt sluggish and even more skittish than before. Customers bought books from her seasonal display, eager to be entertained or even frightened by the stories. Everyone seemed thrilled that October 31st was less than a week away. Not Alice. For the first time in her life, she looked forward to Halloween being over. No more creepy ghosts swaying in the wind, no more pumpkins grinning wickedly at her, no more haunted houses.

"Hey, Alice," Ona said, coming through the door as Alice was getting ready to close, "ready to go visit Dr. Fantasma's haunted house?"

Alice groaned. "Not the haunted house."

Ona gave her a long, probing stare. "You look tired. If you're not feeling up to it, we can do something else."

Alice looked down at the counter. Her copy of *Jabberwocky* lay there, open to where she'd been reading it.

> "Beware the Jabberwock, my son!
> The jaws that bite, the claws that catch!
> Beware the Jubjub bird, and shun
> The frumious Bandersnatch!"

When she'd first read it in *Through the Looking Glass*, "Jabberwocky" had terrified her—but also fascinated her. She couldn't resist reading the disturbing poem again, and again, and again. Which must've been why her mom gifted her a separate book with the poem.

That brought back another memory, something her mom had once said. Alice had come into her mom's bed because of a nightmare, and her mom comforted her: "The bad dream is gone, isn't it? Because you woke up. You opened your eyes, and when you looked at the bad dream it went away. That's the thing about bad dreams. Underneath the frightening masks, they're scaredy cats. Look them straight in the eye and—whoosh—they fly away."

Alice had braved worse things than bad dreams. She wouldn't let a few goosebumps stop her. She'd look those bad dreams straight in the eye.

She shut the *Jabberwocky* book.

"I'm fine," she told Ona. "Let's go see that haunted house."

Outside on Main Street, Alice got into Ona's pickup truck.

"Is Becca joining us?"

"She's working," Ona said.

Enough said. Since Becca's explosion at Stewart Conway, she'd been her usual friendly, garrulous self, but if her dial was usually set to 7, she seemed to have turned it up to 10, moving across the diner with a frenetic energy that was almost as disturbing as her brandishing a steak knife.

And worse yet, the What the Dickens Diner seemed emptier and quieter every day.

"I wish more people would support the diner," she muttered as the pickup moved down Main Street.

Ona sighed. "Yesterday, I felt so angry at the folks who were eating at Gretchen's place. But is that fair? A lot of people are trying to make ends meet. A cheap deal is attractive."

"But what happens if Becca goes out of business? They wouldn't like that, would they? It's like with my bookstore. I can't compete with online stores and their low prices. If no one ever bought a physical book, I'd have to close Wonderland. Maybe I'm flattering myself, but I think people would miss having a bookstore in Blithedale."

"They would," Ona said. "And they'd miss having Becca's diner."

They lapsed into silence, the weight of the problem hanging heavy between them. They didn't need to tell each other how worried they still were about their friend. Alice quietly promised to give more thought to how she could help Becca—this couldn't continue forever.

Something's got to give...

At the fork in Main Street, a wooden-staked sign for the haunted house pointed south. As Ona turned the pickup, Alice glanced at the Darn Good Diner, its brightly lit interior half empty.

"At least Gretchen isn't busy, either," she mumbled.

"Half of Blithedale is at the grand opening of the haunted house," Ona said. "But I bet her diner will be packed again later tonight."

The road twisted and curved as it drove a wedge between the trees. Soon, though, the trees leaned further and further over, creating the illusion of a tunnel and shutting out the last remaining light of the day.

The pickup's headlights flashed across the blacktop. The red lights of another car appeared up ahead, and beyond that, another car. They followed the other vehicles, and before long, they all turned and pulled into a gravel parking lot already packed with cars.

Ona swung the pickup into a space near the road and they got out. Alice peered up at the haunted house. Dr. Fantasma couldn't have picked a better site for his show.

At the top of Stewart Conway's property stood an old Victorian with a shingle roof and a sagging gable and a crooked turret. A rusty weather vane swung back and forth. Oddly, the windows on one half of the house were covered with blinds or even plywood boards, the other half curtained and dark. It gave the house a lopsided look.

Alice pointed it out to Ona.

"In past years, Dr. Fantasma's used the entire house to do the show," Ona said. "But his troupe has gotten smaller over the years, and I hear they now have to block off half the property to keep the show contained."

Flickering jack-o'-lanterns flanked the pathway leading to the house's wraparound porch. Alice and Ona joined the stream of people heading toward the entrance. Dr. Fantasma, wearing his usual formal wear and cloak, stood on the porch, welcoming people with a theatrical flourish.

"Step right this way…don't be afraid…don't be afraid yet, my dears, not yet…ah, good evening, ladies." He bowed to Alice and Ona. "I'm delighted to see you tonight. Your experience awaits you in the west wing of the house. That's up the stairs and to the right. May you have a fun-filled and frightening evening."

Alice linked arms with Ona as they walked inside.

"I hope it's more fun than frightening," she said.

"Amen," Ona said.

In the vestibule, a big staircase rose to a landing, with steps leading upward to a landing, and then twisting back and rising again.

As Alice and Ona ascended, Alice spotted familiar faces ahead of them: Mayor MacDonald in his white Mark Twain suit and cane; the librarian, Lorraine, and her giant friend, Sandy; Esther from the consignment store, Love Again, chatting to Andrea, owner of the Bonsai & Pie cafe; Mr. and Mrs. Oriel, an older couple who, in their matching glasses and clothes, looked oddly identical; Thor, the handsome owner of the Woodlander Bar; Chief of Police James Sapling Jr.—or Jimbo, as everyone called him; and near the top, a familiar blue trench coat. Stewart Conway was talking to a pair of young women from out of town, guests at the inn, no doubt trying to charm them.

A flash of red caught Alice's eye. A few steps behind Conway came Gretchen Tusk, climbing the stairs alone. With her eyes fixed straight ahead, she had a grim look on her face, as if this haunted house were the last place on earth she'd like to be.

"You weren't kidding," Alice said to Ona. "Half of Blithedale is already here."

On the first landing, there were doors to the right and to the left. A sign pointed to the right. A teenager broke free from his friends and ran to the left and grabbed the brass knob of the door and jiggled it.

"Aw, man," he said, and his friends laughed. "Locked."

There was a click, and the door swung inward. The kid jumped back, as if he'd stepped on a snake. From the darkness within, a man emerged. The man Alice had seen threatening Stewart Conway.

"Move on," he snarled.

The kid rejoined his friends, giving the tough guy a backward glance.

Meanwhile, Dr. Fantasma's crew member closed and locked the door behind him. He hurried past Alice and Ona and shouldered his way through the group of teenagers to enter the haunted house experience beyond.

"I'm guessing that guy isn't Dr. Fantasma's public relations expert," Alice said.

Ona said, "I remember him from past years. Duane something. That's it. Duane Rooker. And yeah, he's got the social graces of a grizzly bear."

Alice followed Ona into the haunted house experience, taking a deep breath, expecting the worst.

The first room was decorated to look like a sitting room. Shadows obscured the corners of the room, but flickering lamps on the tables revealed skeletons sitting at a card table, slowly laying out cards, while another leaned against the mantelpiece, smoking a pipe. A piano in a corner seemed to play itself, the keys moving with no help from a person. The tune was the ragtime classic "The Entertainer" by Scott Joplin.

Alice laughed. It was clever how they'd made the skeletons move. They had a lifelike quality that couldn't easily be explained. But they weren't frightening. They reminded Alice of the visual effects from 1940s horror films—or some gag from an Abbott and Costello movie. Definitely more fun than frightening.

As she and Ona moved on to the next room, a rope kept the audience from approaching a stage on which stood a glass cage. And in case the rope wasn't enough of a deterrence, Duane Rooker lurked in the shadows, keeping an eye on the guests. Within the glass cage was what looked like smoke. But every few seconds, the smoke materialized into a ghost, then dispersed again.

It was beautiful, even mesmerizing.

Instead of being frightened, Alice enjoyed speculating with Ona about how Dr. Fantasma and his crew had achieved the various illusions.

They passed through half a dozen rooms with a variety of strange scenes. A cage with a writhing werewolf. A coffin with a hand emerging to open the lid, a very exaggerated scream coming from within. A lab full of beakers with bubbling, colorful liquid and pipettes floating through the air, held by invisible hands. And then they emerged onto the staircase again, following the throng of people upwards to the next landing and through the door to the next set of rooms.

Alice was about to follow Ona inside when she heard a scream.

It sent a frigid chill down her spine and turned her guts to ice.

She froze.

There was nothing theatrical about this scream. It was

genuine horror and shock—and it came from across the landing.

She turned toward the opposite door. The door to the closed-off east wing.

She glanced at Ona, and in an instant the two of them had reached the door.

Alice gripped the doorknob, expecting it to jiggle and do no more. But when she turned the knob and pushed, the door swung inward.

They ran down a gloomy corridor and stumbled into a dark room where a woman stood rooted to the floor— Gretchen Tusk. Heavy black drapes lined the walls. The floorboards were bare, no rugs or furniture. But as Alice took another step into the room, she saw that a man lay on his stomach. Becca stood over him, holding a bloody knife. Her hands were bloody, too.

Gretchen pointed an accusing finger at Becca.

"You killed him," she said, her voice shaky. It must've been her scream that Alice heard. "You killed Stewart."

Another person emerged from the shadowy curtains, seeming to appear from out of nowhere. It was Mrs. Oriel. She said, "Don't be absurd, lady. I saw the killer. It was a ghost that did it. A ghost killed Stewart Conway."

CHAPTER 7

"*H*ow can the diner continue without Becca?" Susan, the waitress at the What the Dickens, swept an arm around to indicate the formica tables and leatherette seats. "I can't possibly manage on my own."

"We'll help," Alice said. "Won't we, Ona?"

Ona nodded. It was rare for her to be so quiet. But since Becca's arrest last night, she'd hardly spoken a word, apparently shocked into silence. Ona didn't need to speak. Alice knew her friend would do what she could to help Susan keep the diner running. They both would.

Alice and Ona sat on stools by the counter. Outside, the morning was chilly, the sky overcast. Glum weather to match the glum mood.

A few early morning patrons had come to the diner, but Susan had suspected them of showing up to get gossip about Becca. She'd chased them out with a spatula.

The handful of people still in the diner looked depressed —locals who knew and loved Becca. Mayor Townsend sat in a booth with Mr. and Mrs. Oriel. Esther and Andrea sat at a table with Thor. A foursome of truckers in their caps and vests hunched over their big breakfasts, eating with an Eeyore-like despondency.

The door opened and Chief Jimbo stepped inside, rubbing his hands and blowing on them. His belt with its flashlight and gun jiggled as he walked across the diner. He was followed by a man in a gray suit so rumpled that it looked as if he'd slept in it. Maybe he had.

Speaking of Eeyore, Alice thought as she recognized Lenny Stout, the county coroner. He was a Winnie-the-Pooh fan, often seen at the diner rereading one of A. A. Milne's classic books. He was also a living embodiment of Eeyore, the downhearted donkey.

"Coffee for two, please?" Chief Jimbo said to Susan, his order more question than statement, and coupled with an uncertain smile. Susan glared daggers at him. But she grabbed two cups and the pot of coffee, bringing them around the counter to where Chief Jimbo and Lenny Stout were taking their seats in a booth.

Chief Jimbo's dad had been the chief of police in Blithedale. As far as Alice knew, James Sapling, Sr. had done a good job of handling law and order in the single-cop town. But his son, Jimbo, was not only a novice; he was poorly suited to the task, as recent crime investigations had proved. Still, Mayor MacDonald kept him in place, and many people in Blithedale shrugged their shoulders and said Jimbo was "all right."

Alice sighed. Chief Jimbo's skills—or lack thereof—made this disaster even worse.

She slipped off her stool and headed over to Chief Jimbo and Lenny. Without being invited, she plonked down on the leatherette seat next to Chief Jimbo.

"Becca didn't kill Stewart Conway," she said. "This whole thing's a misunderstanding. An accident."

"They're funny things, accidents," Lenny said. "You never

have them till you're having them. Though I'd say five stab wounds to the back doesn't look like an accident."

"Becca wasn't the only person in that room."

"Her fingerprints are on the murder weapon. The murder weapon is a steak knife from her own diner—a weapon she used to threaten the victim only days before. The victim's blood is all over her. She was caught alone with the victim around the time of death." Lenny sighed. "Could be worse. Not sure how, but it could be."

"What about Gretchen?"

"And Mrs. Oriel?" Lenny said, raising an eyebrow.

He seemed to know that Alice was unwilling to suspect dear, quirky Mrs. Oriel. But she might be an important witness. Didn't she say that she saw the killer and that it wasn't Becca? After Alice and Ona had stumbled onto the scene, the room had filled with others: Mayor Townsend, Chief Jimbo, Duane Rooker, Andrea, and Esther. Then even Dr. Fantasma had come running, insisting everyone leave the room and let the professionals do their work, his usual theatrics gone. He'd suddenly looked like an ordinary seventy-something-year-old, harried by a horrible tragedy.

And Gretchen? Alice wished she could recall how she'd looked. But her attention had been on Becca, whose wide eyes and deathly pallor had suggested shock. All she'd wanted to do was wrap her arms around her, but Chief Jimbo had demanded that everyone step away—this was a crime scene.

"Well," Alice said, "what about Mrs. Oriel? She said she saw someone."

"Something," Lenny said, taking a sip of coffee. "A ghost."

"It's in my report," Chief Jimbo said with disproportionate pride, as if reports were the greatest challenge he'd faced during the long night. Maybe it was. He was notoriously averse to work, struggling to follow up on the most basic clues.

"That haunted house was full of ghosts," Lenny said. "Besides, Gretchen's statement is damning."

It would be, Alice thought, *wouldn't it?*

It was oh-so convenient that Gretchen caught her rival with blood on her hands. She kept quiet about it, though, waiting for Lenny to say more.

But it was Chief Jimbo who said, "While everyone else was inside the west wing enjoying the show, Gretchen waited outside. She saw Becca on the stairs as she followed Stewart Conway inside the off-limits section of the house. Then found her standing over him with the knife in her hands. That didn't leave anyone much time to kill Conway. Except for Becca, of course."

"I want to see her," Alice said.

"I don't see that it can help," Lenny said.

But Chief Jimbo nodded. "And it can't hurt."

Lenny sighed. "Guess not. It never hurts to keep looking for sunshine, either."

He gestured toward the windows. Alice looked up and saw rain streaking the glass.

CHAPTER 8

*U*nder normal circumstances, the holding cells at the Blithedale Police Department consisted of a concrete ledge in the wall that served as a bed, a metal toilet without a seat, and a metal washstand. But in Becca's cell, the concrete ledge had a camping mattress and sleeping bag on it, and an old TV stood in a corner, the wires running out of the cell.

As Chief Jimbo unlocked the cell, he told Alice and Ona, "Regulations tell me not to place anything in the cell that might aid the prisoner's escape or self-harm. But since Becca's not going to do either, I didn't want her to be uncomfortable."

The TV was playing an episode of Scooby-Doo. Becca looked up as the door swung open.

"Alice? Ona?"

She was on her feet in a flash, and the three women embraced. Alice and Ona held Becca for a long time.

"My diner?" she said, stepping back from them.

"Susan's running things," Ona said. "And we'll help."

"You two—" Becca wiped a tear from her eye. "—you're angels."

Chief Jimbo cleared his throat. "Fifteen minutes. Uh, all right?"

Alice nodded, and Chief Jimbo shut the door and locked it.

Becca sat down on the mattress, and Alice and Ona joined her, sitting on either side of her. For a while, Alice held her friend's hand, giving her time.

Then Becca said, "I didn't kill him."

"We know that." Alice gave Becca's hand a squeeze. "But tell us what happened. You weren't even supposed to be at the haunted house."

Becca shook her head, frowning. "Stewart Conway. I should've known he'd be trouble. See, he and I were lovers. Years ago. He was handsome, charming, swept me off my feet. He made big promises—he was going to invest in an entire chain of diners, buy me a house, take me traveling…" She sighed. "I was having a hard time back then, and I believed him. I wanted to believe him. But soon he left town again, and I realized they'd been lies—part of his story to charm me. He came back to town the next year, and I told him never to talk to me again."

"But he did," Alice said.

"He did. He came to the diner that day, and he tried to charm me again, as if nothing had happened. Under different circumstances, I would've laughed at him and walked away. But I was stressed. I snapped. Then I felt terrible for overre-acting like that. So when he sent me a note asking to set things right, I felt I had to go."

"What note?"

Becca gave Alice a strange look, half worried, half embar-rassed, before digging into her pocket to pull out a square of paper. She unfolded it.

Alice and Ona leaned close. The note had nothing on it.

"Either my one good eye's also out of commission," Ona said, "or that page is blank."

Becca said, "I swear it wasn't when I got it."

Alice believed her. Becca wouldn't lie about a thing like that—or anything, for that matter—and she was the last person Alice could imagine hallucinating. It was possibly the strangest thing she'd ever seen.

She took the paper from Becca and held it up to the fluorescent light and then, finding nothing on it, turned it over. Nothing on the back, either. No other word for it: strange.

"You sure the message was from Conway?"

"He started the message with this term of endearment, 'my little dove.' It was something his Russian grandmother had called him. He talked about setting things right. Asked me to meet him at the haunted house. It sounded like him. Besides, who else would the message have come from?"

Alice and Ona both looked at her.

"Oh," Becca said. "Right. The killer."

"The killer must've wanted you to show up when you did," Alice said. "When you got to the haunted house, what did you see?"

Becca thought for a moment. "People milling around. Dr. Fantasma directed me to the west wing of the house, saying the east was closed. I was on my way up the stairs when I spotted Stewart at the top. He disappeared through a door to the east wing. So I followed him."

"And that was when Gretchen saw you and Stewart. Then what happened?"

"I went down a hallway and came into that room with all the drapes along the walls. I thought I heard moaning. And there he was, lying on the floor. I rushed over and tried to find his pulse, but when I couldn't, I panicked. I grabbed the knife, thinking I could somehow help him, and then I heard a scream. Gretchen was standing there. The rest you know…"

Alice thought about what Becca had told them. The killer must've moved with superhuman speed if they'd killed Conway in the seconds it took Becca to follow him inside.

"You heard moaning?"

"I thought I did. But by the time I got to Stewart, he was dead."

"I bet that wasn't Conway you heard."

"That was the killer?" Becca said, her voice almost a whisper. "The killer was in the room?"

Chief Jimbo appeared at the barred door, jiggling his keys as he unlocked the door. "Sorry," he said, sounding genuinely sorry, "time's up."

Alice and Ona hugged Becca again, and Alice whispered in her ear, "We'll get you out of here. Promise."

At the door, she gave Becca a last look, blowing her a kiss. Then she turned to Chief Jimbo. She had to convince him Becca was innocent. She had to get Becca out.

Chief Jimbo locked the door. Alice and Ona followed him down the corridor and into the police department's open office. There were two desks, only one of which had a computer on it.

Chief Jimbo sat down on the edge of his desk with a heavy sigh.

She considered how to broach the topic with him. He always took the easiest route—and a murder case with a framed suspect didn't sound easy.

Maybe the best approach was to state the obvious first, and then move on from there. She'd give it a shot.

"Listen, Jimbo," Alice began. "Becca's being framed."

"I agree," he said.

Alice stopped. Of all the things he could've said, this was the one thing she hadn't expected. She was aware that she was staring at him with an expression of disbelief. She stared at Ona, who looked just as surprised.

"You agree?"

"Sure, but the problem is," he said, "my book doesn't cover this topic."

He extracted a much-dog-eared paperback from a pocket in his pants: *The Police Chief Companion: 21 Days to Killing It On the Job*. Chief Jimbo lugged that book with him wherever he went and referenced its checklists as if they were scripture.

"Maybe the state police could advise you?" Ona suggested.

Chief Jimbo said, "Those guys don't take me seriously. It'd be like calling my dad in Florida." He shook his head. Then straightened up, looking more confident than usual. "This is my town, my job, and I'll clear Becca's name. Only—"

He sank back into his usual slumped posture.

"Only, it would be great if you could help, Alice."

"Me?"

"You were a big help on the Dorothy Bowers murder case…"

Ona cut in: "And the Vince Malone case."

"Yeah, that one, too." He gave Alice a pleading look, like a kid begging his mom to pretty please do something for him. "And if you could ask around a little, maybe you'd find out who framed Becca…"

Alice couldn't believe it. On the Vince Malone case, Chief Jimbo had refused to believe it was murder, ignoring her when she told him she'd seen the killer flee the scene of the crime. Then, when Dorothy Bowers got killed, Jimbo had gone looking for a serial killer and ignored any evidence that contradicted the idea. Now, he was actually asking her to investigate?

She wasn't sure what to feel. Despair—because

Blithedale's law man would rather leave investigating to a bookseller than do the hard work himself? Or relief—because she wouldn't have to keep her sleuthing a secret from him?

Ona nudged her. "We'll do it, won't we?"

Alice sighed. Her feelings about Chief Jimbo didn't matter. It was Becca, stuck in that cell back there, who mattered.

She nodded. "We'll do it."

"Great!" Chief Jimbo beamed.

"But Jimbo, you mentioned Mrs. Oriel's statement—"

Ona's phone pinged, and she raised it to read the message, then cursed, using language that certainly never appeared in any Jane Austen book Alice had read.

"What's wrong?"

"That big group of city slickers I booked?"

"The party of eight?"

Ona nodded. "Esther just texted me. She spotted them from down the street. They just arrived at the inn."

"And you're not at the inn."

"And the beds aren't made, and fresh towels aren't laid out—the rooms aren't ready at all."

CHAPTER 9

*A*lice and Ona rushed back to the inn. They'd walked to the police department. One benefit of Blithedale being so small. But it meant that Ona's pickup stood parked at the inn, and they had to make a run for it.

By the time they reached Old Mayor Townsend's ghostly statue and bolted up the path to the front porch, Alice was panting.

She expected the lobby to be crowded with the party of eight. But it was empty. A cardboard sign stood on the reception with a message in an elegant curlicue:

> Welcome to the Pemberley Inn. Your refreshments await you in the lounge. We will fetch you soon to show you to your rooms.

"Nice—" Alice sucked in air. "Nice touch."

Ona shook her head as she leaned against the staircase's balustrade, trying to catch her breath, too.

"I didn't write that."

Sounds drifted to them from the back. Music. Voices. Someone laughing. They followed the sounds down the hallway to the back of the old mansion, where the inn's lounge looked out over the backyard. The windows provided a good view of the dozens of tiny houses that Ona had built —a veritable village of tiny houses—but it wasn't that familiar sight that made Alice stop at the threshold to the lounge. Ona stopped, too, clearly as surprised.

The party of eight sat in the armchairs and sofas, looking comfortable. Music played on the lounge's sound system. On a coffee table sat a tray with a pitcher of lemonade, a thermos of coffee, a pot of tea, cups, plates, spoons, cake forks, and a platter heaped with brownies.

"Huh," Ona said.

Curiouser and curiouser, Alice thought.

One of the guests looked up at them and smiled. "Hi," he said, and Ona, snapping out of her surprise, stepped forward to greet her guests. One of them said, "Love the fresh-made brownies." Another said, "Perfect start to our Halloween getaway from the city." Then she added, "Are the rooms ready?"

Ona visibly stiffened. Alice put a hand on her shoulder to calm her. She muttered, "Give me 15 minutes."

"I'll stall," Ona said out the side of her mouth. Then, in a louder voice for the benefit of the group: "First, let me tell you about what's happening in Blithedale over Halloween…"

Alice turned and strolled out of the lounge. Once she was out of eyesight, she broke into a run. She stopped at the front desk first, checking Ona's computer to see which rooms the guests were booked into. Once she had the room keys stuffed into her back pocket, she sprinted to the cupboards with the linen, grabbing stacks of sheets. She found fresh towels, too. And the soft, white bathrobes with "Pemberley Inn" stitched on the front. The pile in her arms grew tall, almost too tall to carry.

She staggered down the corridor to the nearest rooms.

She put down the pile of linen and towels and fumbled with the keys until she found the right one. She slotted the key into the door and prayed—hoped and prayed—that the room didn't also look visibly dirty.

The lock clicked, and she pushed the door inward. She grabbed the sheets and towels she needed and headed inside, ready to make the bed in record time and—

She stopped. And stared.

"What the—?!"

She opened the bathroom door. Then looked at the bed again. She almost felt the inclination to rub her eyes or pinch herself to confirm this wasn't a dream.

Someone had made the bed. Clean sheets stretched over the mattress, carefully tucked in. Fresh towels rested on top of the bedspread. The bathroom was spotless. Trash cans empty. Everything ready for the guests.

As it should be.

Except it should've been messy, unmade, a complete disaster.

Behind her, Ona appeared in the doorway. "Wow, that was quick."

"I didn't do this," Alice said.

They checked the next room, and the room after that. All the beds were made, fresh towels and bathrobes laid out, everything clean and tidy.

"Am I going crazy?" Ona said.

"If you are," Alice said, "I am, too."

CHAPTER 10

That night, Alice woke to the creaking of floorboards and sat bolt upright, her heart beating fast.

She thought, *In the attic...*

But this time, the sound came from outside her door. Then there was a knock. Ona whispered, "Alice, Alice, wake up."

Her voice was urgent, and it sent Alice scrambling out of bed, throwing off the covers and rushing across the floorboards. She unlocked the door and threw it open.

Ona stood outside in one of her Regency-period night-gowns, an eye-patch over her eye without her trademark rhinestones.

"Quick," she said. "Someone's creeping around the backyard."

Alice threw on a bathrobe and, anticipating they'd have to go outside, shoved on a pair of sneakers.

Down the stairs they went. Ona expertly trod at the edges of the steps, ensuring they creaked as little as possible, and Alice followed suit. When they reached the bottom, Ona grabbed her arm and leaned close to whisper as they moved down the hallway.

"I heard sounds from within the house. Maybe a guest wandering around. It happens. Some people can't sleep and they go to the lounge. But when I checked to see if I could offer hot cocoa, there was no one in the lounge. And then I spotted someone creeping around the backyard. I'm sure it's not a guest."

They reached the lounge. Like the rest of the house, it was dark, though Ona had installed dim nightlights in the hallway to make it easy for guests to find their way if, as she'd explained, they struggled to sleep.

As Ona had said, the lounge was empty.

"Look," Ona said, and wriggled the handle to one of the French doors leading to the back. The door didn't budge.

"It's locked." Alice shrugged. "So?"

"So, if it's a sleepless guest roaming the backyard, this door should be open." She gasped and grabbed Alice's arm. "There."

Alice followed her gaze. Outside, the tiny houses made a shadowy village under the overcast night sky. Occasionally, the scudding clouds unveiled the moon, and the windows and eaves brightened. So did a figure moving among the houses.

But only for an instant. If Ona hadn't pointed the person out, Alice might have doubted her own senses.

"Let's go look," she said.

Ona nodded and opened the back door.

Icy air rushed in, and Alice pulled her bathrobe tight around her. Ona shivered. Alice said, "Go get a coat. I'll meet you down there."

Ona nodded, turned, and tiptoed back inside. Alice continued down the steps to the backyard, heading for the area where she'd spotted the intruder.

A path cut straight down the middle of the village of tiny houses. The small buildings stood arranged in concentric circles, fanning out from a clearing in the middle. Ona had her showroom there. It meant that Alice had a clear view of the "village square" up ahead. But on either side, the paths curved around the tiny houses, obscuring anything—or anyone—concealed behind them.

There were tiny houses that looked like log cabins, Nantucket-style homes, miniature castles, gingerbread houses, even one inspired by Bag End, Bilbo's home in *The Hobbit*.

Alice was a few paces from the clearing at the center when a movement out of the corner of her eye caught her attention, and she spun toward it. A flash of white. A figure sweeping away.

"Hey!" she called out, and ran ahead, then turned right, hoping to cut off the person.

But as she rounded the corner of a tiny house, she heard something to her left. She turned and saw a flash of white from across the way.

She stopped. As she turned to pursue the person in that direction, she heard footsteps behind her. She whipped around, just in time to see another flash of white as someone flew from between one cluster of tiny houses to another.

She rushed forward, determined to catch the intruder. But heard steps behind her. There was the person again, gliding among the tiny houses. But all the way across the central clearing. How could a human being move so fast? It was impossible...

Unless...

She pushed the thought aside and sprinted toward the place where she'd seen the intruder. A white apparition came out of nowhere, a sudden flash, and then they collided with a hard whomp. It knocked the breath out of her. But she scrambled to grab the person, keep them from running, and—

"Alice," Ona hissed. "It's me."

Alice stopped struggling. She was holding Ona in her arms. Ona, in her white Regency nightgown and a white puffer jacket, had looked like an apparition.

"I saw someone," Alice said, as she stepped back from her friend. In her mind, she added, *Or something*. "They were over there. Then over there. And then—"

"There!"

Ona pointed. A figure in white floated from behind one tiny to house to another, vanishing. Alice and Ona gave chase. But when they reached the clearing, Ona said, "No, over there," pointing to the apparition, which had somehow reappeared near the back steps of the inn.

Alice suspected the intruder would only disappear and then reappear halfway across the backyard again. So she spun around. "You go that way, Ona. I'll go this way."

Ona nodded.

They darted off in opposite directions, Alice moving toward the back of the property. As she moved further and further away from the inn, she came closer and closer to the back fence. Behind the fence rose tall trees—the Blithedale Woods—and off to the right, she could hear the rushing of the Hiawatha River.

Behind her, she heard Ona call out, "Wait—stop!"

Alice resisted the temptation to go back. Every time she'd come close to the intruder—or apparition, if that was what it was—it had popped up elsewhere. Maybe with Ona chasing it down at the other end, it would turn up near the back.

She crept around a tiny house with half-timbered walls and a thatched roof, like something from Grimm's Fairy Tales, and then saw the apparition. It was near the back fence, and as the clouds parted and moonlight flooded the scene, the figure seemed to rise into the air, floating toward the night sky.

Alice drew in a sharp breath, frozen to the spot. Her mind seemed to freeze, too, unable to make sense of what she saw. Then the clouds rolled over the moon, dispelling the illusion. The person wasn't flying; they were climbing the fence.

She bolted forward. The intruder had almost reached the top. They threw a leg over, straddling the fence.

"Hey, you!" Alice called out.

Just as the intruder turned, surprised by her voice, the moon made another appearance. It cast a sheen of white light across his face—*his, not its*—before the young man swung over the other side and scrambled down.

An instant later, she heard him crashing through the undergrowth.

Then he was gone.

But she'd gotten a good look at him. That was no ghost climbing the Pemberley Inn's back fence. That was Gretchen's chef from the Darn Good Diner.

CHAPTER 11

In the morning, Alice and Ona went to the diner, drank coffee, and ate eggs and toast. Afterward, they strapped on aprons to help Susan during the breakfast rush. As they shuttled plates of bacon and eggs and pots of coffee back and forth, they occasionally managed to snatch a conversation at the counter.

"What was Gretchen's chef doing at the inn last night?" Ona wondered.

"No idea."

"I swear, I was convinced he was a ghost. The way he moved. Have you ever seen someone move so fast?"

"Not outside a skating rink."

Mayor MacDonald was sitting at a table with the Oriels. As Alice refilled their coffee cups, she caught Mrs. Oriel saying, "Becca didn't touch that guy."

"Well, she was holding that knife," Mayor MacDonald said.

"The knife." Mrs. Oriel snorted. "The knife's not the important thing."

"Then what is?" Alice asked, pausing in her duties as a waitress.

Mrs. Oriel gave her a knowing look. "The ghost."

Alice sighed. She'd had enough ghosts to last a lifetime already. But if Mrs. Oriel sensed her impatience, she didn't let on. She continued: "I saw the ghost that killed Mr. Conway."

Alice thought of the "ghost" last night at the inn. That was the kind of ghost who left footprints and fingerprints. Maybe Mrs. Oriel's ghost did, too.

"What exactly did you see, Mrs. Oriel?"

"I was looking for a restroom. There was one downstairs, apparently, but I didn't want to miss the show, so I took a look in the east wing."

"But the doors to the east wing were locked."

"Not when I tried. I left Mr. Oriel—" She nodded at her husband, who smiled. "—and headed down a corridor in the east wing. I heard a noise, which made me turn down another. I went through a couple of rooms and suddenly wondered whether I'd taken a left or a right back there. I was a little lost. But then I heard the sound again. So I followed it. I came to a door that led to a set of narrow stairs. It must've been the servants' entrance long ago. I climbed them, went through another door, down a corridor, through more rooms, and every time I thought I was lost, I heard that noise. Stepping through a door, I got tangled in a set of curtains. Finally, I found a way through, and there it was."

She paused.

Alice said, "What was?"

"The ghost," Mrs. Oriel said. "Floating over a dead man."

She stared at Alice, apparently waiting for her to react.

"Well," Alice said, "what did you do?"

"I thought I'd somehow made my way back to the west wing. After all, this must be a scene from the show. So I turned around. I tried to find my way out again—and that was when I heard someone scream. It didn't sound like pretend. So I ran back. It was Gretchen screaming, and Becca was holding the knife."

"But the body on the floor…"

"It was Mr. Conway, of course. Only when I first saw him, I didn't realize it."

"And the ghost? Who was the ghost?"

"Oh, it was a ghoulish-looking ghost, definitely long dead, and furious-looking. It was floating about a foot above the floor."

"Floating?" Alice asked. "Above the floor?"

"About a foot above it. And the ghost was transparent."

"You're sure?"

"Nothing wrong with my eyes. Or my glasses."

Mr. Oriel interjected. "We go to the optician regularly. Our prescriptions are up to date. Never had a problem, either. And we've seen ghosts before."

"More than once before," Mrs. Oriel said, nodding. "But rarely one so foul-looking."

"Like a monster from the grave."

"Not a monster, my dear. Monsters are different. Corporeal."

"True, true," Mr. Oriel said. "But *like* a monster."

"Oh, yes. Like a monster. A monstrous, immaterial ghoul. Not a friendly ghost at all. Not like the old colonel we once saw…"

Mr. Oriel chuckled. "Ah, the old colonel…what a pleasant ghost."

A nearby table called for more coffee, and Alice moved away, leaving Mr. and Mrs. Oriel to discuss the various ghosts they'd seen, Mayor MacDonald placidly eating his scrambled eggs and drinking his coffee, with only the hint of a wry smile on his lips.

Mrs. Oriel had seen the killer. Alice didn't doubt it. Plus, she'd confirmed that Conway was dead before Becca arrived. But it was bad luck that it had been kooky Mrs. Oriel who would turn out to be Becca's best witness. She also didn't doubt Mrs. Oriel could've seen someone looking like a ghost —but a *floating* ghost?

She recalled her own confusion last night. For a moment, the young man climbing the fence had looked as if he were levitating. Then Alice had realized what she was really seeing.

But Mrs. Oriel didn't seem in doubt.

Shortly after she'd seen the ghost, Becca would've arrived, followed by Gretchen. The room was otherwise bare. Could the killer have been suspended on wires from the ceiling? But that didn't account for the ghost being see-through. And how did a see-through ghost stab a man in the back?

Alice filled coffee cups as she considered the problem. But Susan grabbed her by the arm and interrupted her thoughts.

"Alice, can you take the booth back there? If I have to deal with that old con artist one more time, I swear I'll knock his teeth out."

Alice followed Susan's gesture and saw Dr. Fantasma sitting in a booth with his crew. If anyone could answer her questions about ghosts, it ought to be him.

She headed over to the booth.

"Dr. Fantasma," she said. "What can I get you all to eat and drink?"

Dr. Fantasma smiled. "Kids? What sustenance do you desire this morning?"

Duane Rooker leaned over a menu, a scowl on his face. "Pancakes. Scrambled eggs. Coffee."

He pushed the menu away and sat back, arms across his chest.

The young woman across from him had better manners. She said, "I'll have the oatmeal and a cup of tea, please."

"And I'll have the English muffin with two soft-boiled eggs," Dr. Fantasma said. "And a glass of orange juice."

As Alice gathered up the menus, she tried to sound casually interested as she said, "I thought your haunted house experience was excellent. One trick I was wondering about was the floating ghost. How did you do it?"

"We didn't have a floating ghost," Duane said, scowling at her.

"My mistake," Alice said. "But if you did, how would it work?"

Before Duane could answer, Dr. Fantasma said, "We never divulge the tricks of the trade. Do we, Duane?"

"Mrs. Oriel saw a ghost—"

"And when I am a ghost, you may ask me in a seance. Duane and I will take the secrets of our show to the grave with us."

Alice felt irritation rise into anger, heat spreading up her neck. "Listen, we're dealing with an innocent woman being framed for murder, and you're protecting a bunch of magic tricks?"

"So much more than magic tricks, my dear."

"It's entertainment," Alice said. "I'm talking about justice."

"Oh, you pour salt on my wounds. But even salt—" He picked up the salt shaker and clenched his other fist and poured salt into it, a long stream of white granules. "—can disappear."

He opened his fist. The salt was gone.

"Where did it go?" he asked, staring at his open palm, then clenching it into a fist again.

"I don't know," Alice said. "And I don't care."

"Leave her alone, Doc," the young woman said.

"Yeah, cut it out," Duane grumbled.

Ignoring them, Dr. Fantasma gestured for her to come close. She leaned in. He whispered, "But you should care. Maybe the magic salt won't answer your question about the ghost. But the pepper will."

He opened his hand. It was full of pepper.

Alice let out a huff of irritation. She clenched her fists. "I've had enough of your riddles and tricks—"

Ona swept past, threw an arm around Alice's shoulders, and pulled her away.

"He refuses to talk," Alice said.

"All right," Ona said. "If he won't talk, maybe the scene of the crime will. Tonight."

They looked at each other. Someone was calling for a coffee refill. Someone else asked for more maple syrup.

"It's a date," Alice told Ona, and she turned to bring coffee to a nearby table. As she glanced back at Dr. Fantasma, he winked at her.

CHAPTER 12

*A*fter a couple of hours at the diner, Alice and Ona left Susan to tend to the few remaining customers. Ona headed back to the inn while Alice opened the bookstore. Before parting, though, they agreed to meet at the inn later. Then, after helping Susan with the dinner rush, they would head back to the haunted house to take another look at the scene of the crime.

Alice tried to shake off her frustration at Dr. Fantasma. How could he continue to play the part of the wizard when there had been a murder? When Becca was locked up for a crime she didn't commit? His playfulness, which had seemed delightful before, now seemed selfish.

Once she got busy restocking shelves and dealing with customers, though, her annoyance melted away. A dad with his twin five-year-old daughters came into the store to buy Halloween books, and watching him introduce them to new books warmed Alice. The girls left with a bag full of books and such giddy excitement that Alice couldn't resist grinning.

Maybe not all people are selfish...

In the afternoon, Alice was surprised to see the young woman from Dr. Fantasma's crew come into the bookstore. She pushed an elderly woman in a wheelchair up the ramp and into the tiny house. The woman wore a striking outfit of red and black—a black dress with a red scarf slung around her neck.

"Hi, again," the young woman said.

"You're with Dr. Fantasma."

"I'm Holly."

"And I'm—"

"Mrs. Hartford," the old woman interrupted. "I don't forget a face, and, hold on a minute, where is that sweet girl of yours?"

As the woman looked around the shop, a hand squeezed Alice's heart.

My God, she thinks I'm Mom...

Holly leaned over the woman and said in a gentle voice, "Mom, this isn't who you think it is."

Holly's mom looked confused as she gazed at Alice.

"But I recognize you…"

Alice came around the counter. "You recognize me for a reason. You recognized my mom in me. But I'm not Mrs. Hartford. I'm her daughter, Alice."

"Alice," the woman said, almost like letting out a sigh. But there was uncertainty in her eyes. "I remember. And I remember the bookstore. Except the way I remember it, it was much bigger."

"Well, this is a different bookstore. My mom's bookstore is gone. I built this one on the same lot. My store is half the size."

"But twice as cozy," Holly said. "We like cozy, don't we, Mom?"

The old woman smiled up at her daughter. "And books. We love books."

They spoke for a while longer, Holly explaining that her mom had been an English teacher, and still loved books more than anything.

"Not more than you," the old woman said.

Holly took her mom's hand and squeezed it, while tears welled in her eyes. She looked away.

Sensing Holly needed a change of topic, Alice asked them what they'd like to read.

"I read books aloud to my mom now," Holly said. "Ever since…" She didn't finish her sentence. "Reading is hard for her now."

Alice nodded, trying to convey that they didn't need to talk about it if Holly didn't want to. Clearly, Holly's mom was ill, and it was taking its toll on the daughter. It was difficult for Alice to leave her own experience out of it. Her mom had been much younger when she got sick. But she felt for Holly —losing your mom at any age was hard.

"How about some Halloween stories?" Alice suggested, gesturing toward her books on display. "Do you like ghost stories? Gothic stories? That kind of thing?"

"As long as they don't involve attics," Holly said, and shuddered. "Ever since I read *Jane Eyre* at a very young age, attics have terrified me."

"Worse than cellars?"

"Cellars don't seem so bad. I always think of cellars as ideal for absent-minded professors concocting potions or cobbling together clever machines."

That made Alice think of Dr. Fantasma. What kinds of clever machines did Dr. Fantasma cobble together—ones that could make ghosts fly?

Alice recommended a few books. Holly's mom wanted her daughter to read Wilkie Collins' *The Woman in White* to her. The old woman admired the edition Alice found for them. Meanwhile, Holly explained that her mom lived in Blithedale.

"It's been hard to live a life on the road with Dr. Fantasma when my mom needs me here. She lives alone, but increasingly needs help. That's why I'll have to stay in Blithedale, and somehow figure out how to move my career here."

"That sounds difficult," Alice said.

Holly shrugged. "It's not easy. But we'll manage. I'm trying to do right by my mom while also doing right by myself. Speaking of which, I'd love some advice as I figure out how to set up a business. Practical things. Like insurance. Got any recommendations?"

Alice shared what she learned from setting up her own business—legal entities, personal liability, taxes, cash flow, business plans—and they passed a good 20 minutes in pleasant conversation. Alice recommended the insurance company she herself had chosen.

Then said, "You need personal insurance, too?"

"I've got life insurance already. My one big expense. See, my mom depends on me, and if anything were to happen to me..."

"Nothing's going to happen to you, sweetie," her mom said.

Holly reached down and took her mom's hand and squeezed it.

Her mom smiled up at her. "You and I have some reading to do."

Besides the Wilkie Collins book, Holly's mom had picked out a beautiful edition from Virago Press of Daphne du Maurier's *The Birds and Other Stories*. The cover design consisted of red bird-like geometric patterns on a black background.

"Red and black—my favorite colors," the old woman said and smiled at Alice.

After they left, Alice leaned against her counter and let out a long sigh. Dr. Fantasma's behavior had upset her. But other people didn't share his attitude. The world was full of people doing their best to care for the ones they loved.

CHAPTER 13

*A*fter closing the bookstore, Alice joined Ona at the inn, and helped her prepare snacks and refreshments for guests who'd been out hiking the whole day. They left a tray with four thermoses on the table: two with coffee —one regular and one decaf; one with tea; and the last with hot chocolate. They also left a bowl of cookies and another with apple slices. And finally, a big pitcher of water.

"No ghosts to leave out coffee and cake today?" Alice asked.

"Maybe they're leprechauns. Maybe they only come out when you really need them."

"Hmm...so, can we ask the leprechauns to help us get Becca out of this fix?"

Ona went to the nearest bookshelf and picked up a little antique bell.

"Leprechauns—did you hear that?" She rang the bell. "We'd like your help to prove Becca's innocent."

She rang the bell again.

In the distance, a bell dinged.

Alice and Ona looked at each other, Ona's one visible eye

going wide. Alice felt a prickling all over her back. Her shoulders tensed.

"Was that…?" she whispered.

The bell dinged again.

Ona snorted. "Ha. The reception desk bell."

Alice relaxed, and a wave of laughter escaped her.

"All this ghost stuff is making me crazy."

"Me, too."

Ona put an arm around her, and together they headed down the hallway toward the reception desk. A woman stood by the desk, a suitcase by her side. She was dressed in a long camel coat and tall brown boots. Her leather gloves matched the outfit. She wore pearl earrings.

"I'm so sorry," Ona said, smiling, "but we're fully booked."

"You've got a room that's empty. Stewart Conway's."

Ona's smile faltered. "Yes, but—"

"I don't believe the police require you to keep it locked up, do they?"

"That's true, but his things are—"

"His things are mine now. I'm Peyton Conway, his wife."

Ona glanced at Alice, apparently struggling to find the right words.

Alice said, "Mrs. Conway. We're so sorry for your loss. And I'm happy to give up my room, since the only one available was your husband's."

Mrs. Conway slipped off the leather gloves, one finger at a time, seemingly unruffled by the conversation.

"Thanks," she said. "Truth is, he was a jerk. A terrible husband."

She finished taking her gloves off.

"As for the room, I appreciate the offer. You're very kind."

She smiled at Alice, and Alice got the impression of a woman who was bone weary, and despite her brusque manner, not unsympathetic to others.

"Look, ladies, I'm not unnerved by sleeping in the same bed my husband did. It was considerably harder to muster it when he was alive. And in case you're worried about him haunting me, please don't. I don't believe in ghosts and goblins, and the only devil I ever met was the one I married."

Ona handed her the key to Stewart Conway's room.

"Here you go, Mrs. Conway."

"Peyton, please. I prefer it."

Alice and Ona introduced themselves, offering their first names, too. Then Ona walked Peyton through the house to show her the room. Peyton complimented Ona on her beautiful inn and asked questions about its history. Their voices faded as they disappeared deeper into the house.

Alice stayed at the reception desk, reflecting on how people could surprise you. She also thought of Ona's luck in filling the entire inn. There was only one room that didn't bring her any income: Alice's suite.

She remembered what Holly had said about doing right by her mom and by herself. That was the ideal, wasn't it? To find that balance between doing right by others while doing right by yourself.

Wonderland Books was doing well. Better than well, in fact. When Alice had moved into the Pemberley Inn, she couldn't afford to stay at a hotel week after week. But things had changed.

On a shelf below the reception counter, she found an envelope. She checked the price of the Colonel Brandon Suite and stuffed a wad of twenty-dollar bills into the envelope. Then wrote on the outside:

For Ona: I'm paying my rent. So I can stay at the Pemberley forever.

She drew a smiley face underneath and signed it, then stuffed it into the cash register. When she straightened up, Mayor MacDonald was coming through the front door.

He wore his usual white Mark Twain suit. It matched his white hair and mustache, making him the perfect candidate for a Mark Twain lookalike competition.

"I've got an appointment with one of the guests," he said.

"Cultivating new clients?"

He nodded. Mayor MacDonald ran the town's only realty firm, giving him a near monopoly on the real estate market.

"And here she is now," he said, smiling.

Peyton Conway came down the hallway, with Ona by her side. Peyton smiled at Mayor MacDonald.

"Good to see you, mayor," she said. "Ready for a drink?"

"Always," Mayor MacDonald said. "It goes well with business."

Alice, curious, asked Peyton, "Are you planning to move to Blithedale?"

She shook her head. "Unfortunately, not. But I am selling that old Victorian that my husband rented out to Dr. Fantasma."

"The haunted house?"

"Yes. Every haunted house Stewart owned—I'm selling them all."

CHAPTER 14

$\mathcal{U}$nder the light of the moon, the house looked dark and hollow.

But rotten logs are hollow, Alice thought, *and they can be full of creepy, crawly things.*

She hugged herself, telling herself it was the cold that made her shudder.

The dinner rush at the diner had lasted longer than expected, and it was late. Ona crouched next to her. Her pickup truck stood parked down the street. They concealed themselves behind trees, scoping out the scene to make sure they were alone.

Ona said, "Tell me this is a stupid idea and we should turn around and go back. I'm willing to be convinced."

Alice shook her head. "It's just a spooky old house. The only thing to fear is—"

"Yeah, I know, I know, *fear itself.*"

"I was thinking of *failure*. If we fail, Becca may end up in prison for murder."

Ona nodded. "You're right. Let's go."

Alice glanced over her shoulder and scanned the area

ahead again. No sign of life. The gravel and grass that had served as the parking lot were empty. The woods were as a still as the house, the shadowy trees as gray as fossils in the moonlight.

They came out of the trees and moved up the drive. It couldn't be more than twenty yards from where they'd hidden, but it felt as if she was trying to tiptoe across a football field.

In bright stadium lights, with the bleachers in darkness, and someone up there watching.

Her gut twisted, but she reminded herself that it must be nothing compared to how Becca felt.

At the front porch, Alice said, "Let's see if there's a back entrance. Or maybe someone forgot to close a window. We can climb in."

Ona climbed the porch steps to the front door and reached for the doorknob. She turned it and pulled open the door. It creaked on its hinges.

"Well, that was lucky," she said. "Front door's open."

"Yeah, lucky."

Alice didn't like it. A locked house meant an undisturbed house. Still, it was the easiest way inside, and the sooner they got another look at the crime scene, the sooner they could head back home. She followed Ona into the gloom.

Inside, Alice waited for her eyes to adjust to the darkness. The staircase loomed up from the floorboards, stretching into shadow. Vague outlines of wainscoting and ornately framed portraits formed along the walls as she took her first steps upward. Except as she drew closer, she saw that there were no portraits, only the ghostly outlines of where they had once hung.

The shadows are playing tricks on me.

Ona was right behind her. They walked at the edge of the staircase where their footfall was least likely to set off creaks and groans. But it was impossible to avoid. Each time the stairs complained, it sent a chill down Alice's back.

On the first landing, Ona tried the door to the west wing.

"Locked," she whispered.

Alice went to the east wing door, a horrible feeling in the pit of her stomach. It would be unlocked. It would lead them to something terrible.

She turned the doorknob. The door rattled in its frame.

She let out a sigh. "Locked."

Alice turned to continue upward. Then froze when she saw someone standing at the top of the stairs.

On the landing above, a man in a trench coat stared into space. He hovered a foot or so above the carpeted floor and he was as insubstantial as fog. But she recognized him.

"Stewart Conway…"

Goosebumps crawled all over her skin.

And then he spoke, his voice thin and as wispy as his spectral body, like an old radio that was all treble and no bass.

"What have I done to deserve this? Why punish me for falling in love?" He extended his hands in a ghostly plea. "Please, my little dove…please."

The words jolted her.

Becca, she thought, and that thought broke her free from her paralysis. She put a foot on the first stair. Ghost or not, this apparition was a clue to who killed Stewart Conway, and she wouldn't let fear of the otherworldly hold her back.

She was about to launch herself upward when, downstairs, the front door gave a crack, and it creaked open. Footfall on the steps, the old boards creaking and groaning, and then:

"Hello…?" A tentative voice. "Anyone there…?"

Alice turned and looked down the stairs. Ona did, too. Chief Jimbo appeared out of the darkness, a worried look on his face. He seemed to shrink from the shadows along the staircase. When he saw Alice and Ona, though, his face brightened.

"Oh, you two are here," he said. "Thank goodness."

Then he looked up and saw the ghost and his face went pale. He staggered back against the wall.

"G—g—g—ghost," he spluttered.

Conway's specter repeated what he'd said before: "What have I done to deserve this? Why punish me for falling in love? Please, my little dove…please."

Something about Chief Jimbo's presence—or maybe it was Conway repeating his plea word for word—broke the spell entirely, and Alice whipped around to inspect this so-called apparition.

As she turned, she came face to face with a man.

She let out a yelp.

Duane Rooker stood only an arm's length from her. He must've come out of the door to the west wing without her hearing.

She said, "Jeez, you scared me half to death."

"This is private property," he said. "You're trespassing."

"So is he," Alice said, pointing to the landing above.

Duane Rooker looked up. "Who?"

Alice followed his gaze. The landing was empty, shrouded in darkness. She looked toward the end of the landing. Nothing.

"He's gone," she said.

"Who?" Duane repeated.

"Stewart Conway."

Ona added, "The ghost of Stewart Conway."

Duane stared at them, a frown on his face. Then the frown deepened to disgust. "Get out of here. I give you five seconds. Get out. And if either of you says anything ridiculous about ghosts again, I'll drag you out."

Alice gestured toward the landing. "But we saw—"

"You people think because we do these haunted house shows that we're gullible. Likely to believe anything. Easily taken in by stories about ghosts and ghouls."

Chief Jimbo said, "I think I really did see—"

"Enough." Duane squared his jaw. Alice had seen friendlier-looking bouncers at dive bars. "Five seconds," he growled.

Chief Jimbo made a show of looking at his watch. "Well, look at that. It's later than I thought. I'll talk to you all later."

He made for the stairs, hurrying down.

Alice said, "There's something fishy going on, and I'm going to—"

"Five," Duane said.

"Look, you can't intimidate us—"

"Four."

"We just want to know—"

"Three."

He took a step toward Alice and Ona. He clenched his fists.

"Two."

Ona gripped Alice's hand. She muttered, "I don't need a black eye—I've only got one to spare, remember?"

Alice allowed Ona to pull her toward the steps leading down. At first she resisted, wanting to show Duane they weren't afraid of him. But his cold, hard gaze told her she'd be a fool to confront this guy in a dark place at night, especially since the town's only cop had just excused himself.

"One," Duane called out.

She sped up, and then she and Ona were both bounding down the stairs. They threw themselves out of the front door and stumbled down the front steps and onto the gravel drive. A car stood parked close to the porch. Duane's.

A pair of headlights—no doubt from Chief Jimbo's

cruiser—flashed beyond the trees, disappearing down the road.

Alice and Ona ran for cover. They leaped over roots and rocks and dodged around the giant trunks of trees.

It was only when Alice was sure they were out of sight that she slowed down and grabbed Ona's arm to stop her, too.

They both bent over, panting.

"That coward," Ona said.

"Forget about Chief Jimbo…" Alice huffed. "What was Duane Rooker doing there?"

"See the look—" Ona said, also trying to catch her breath. "—the look in his eyes?"

Alice nodded. "Like a vicious dog."

"Like a killer."

Neither said anything for a while. Ona was right. Duane had a hardness to him that made Alice think he wouldn't be above hurting another human being. But even as her heart pounded in her chest, she pushed her fear of Duane Rooker aside, because there was another, more important thing to consider.

The ghost of Stewart Conway.

She shook her head. "Could that really have been a ghost we saw?"

"What else would it be?"

Alice glanced back up at the house. A light was on in the hallway windows. A shadow moved past a window on the third story—the landing where they'd seen the ghost. That must be Duane moving around up there.

"I'm not sure what we saw," Alice admitted. "But did you hear what Conway said?"

Ona shrugged. "Something about being punished for falling in love."

"Yes, but he wasn't talking to us, was he?"

"He was talking to his long-lost love. Don't ghosts get stuck doing that when death separates them from their loved ones?"

"What did he call the person he was talking to?"

Ona thought for a moment. Then she grabbed Alice's arm.

"'My little dove.'"

Alice nodded. "Which is what he called Becca."

For a while, they stood still among the dark trees. Up at the house, the hallway lights went out. But a moment later, a flash of light spun across a window in the east wing. A flashlight. It seemed Duane Rooker was moving through the big house. Was he searching for something—or someone?

Alice said, "Conway's ghost wanted to tell us something."

"I thought he wanted to tell his lover—Becca—something. What did he say? 'What have I done to deserve this? Why punish me for falling in love? Please, my little dove. Please.'"

"He wasn't there to tell Becca anything. He was there to tell *us*. He wanted to make sure we knew who punished him."

Ona gave her a sharp look. "Becca?"

"That's right. Conway's ghost just confirmed the official story—that Becca murdered him."

CHAPTER 15

"*I* need a drink," Ona said as she steered the pickup down the dark road.

"I was hoping you'd say that," Alice said.

But it was late, and as they drove past the Woodlander Bar, they could see the tiny-house bar was dark and closed up for the night. They kept driving, Ona turning down the main road to town.

The diner would be closed now, too. So would Bonsai & Pie, Andrea's hole-in-the-wall cafe. "Guess we'll hang out at the inn."

"Unless you want to go to the Darn Good Diner."

Ona pointed out the windshield. As they came to the fork in the road where the Darn Good Diner sat, Alice noticed the lights were on. But the parking lot was empty.

"Let's take a look," she said.

Ona turned into the parking lot and they got out of the pickup truck. On the door, the sign said, "Sorry We're Closed." But Alice spotted two familiar heads of purple hair at the counter inside, and she knocked on the glass.

A moment later, the door was unlocked, and Edie grinned at them.

"Come on in."

Edie led them to the stools by the counter and Fleur gave them a little bashful wave as Alice and Ona got comfortable. The delicious smell of food filled the air. Music played on the speakers in the diner—funky jazz with a hip-hop beat—and Dylan, the chef, moved back and forth in the kitchen, preparing food.

When he saw Alice and Ona, he frowned.

"Hey," he said. "We're actually closed."

Edie said, "Chill, Dylan. They're all right."

He stared at Alice and Ona as if studying them. Then nodded and said, "You want to taste some real food?"

Alice's stomach rumbled a loud and clear *yes*. Work at the diner had been so busy that she and Ona hadn't had time for more than a few tortilla chips with some salsa and guacamole. She was famished.

"We'd love to," Ona said, clearly feeling the same way.

What followed was a surprise treat—a series of small plates with inventive and delicious food. There was a thinly sliced Mediterranean chicken baked with cherry tomatoes, olives, and capers; a ramekin of shrimp cooked in olive oil with garlic, which they mopped up with crusty bread; roasted cauliflower drizzled with pomegranate molasses and tahini sauce; tiny crab cakes; miniature Philly cheesesteak sandwiches; and for dessert, a slice of pumpkin pie with homemade whipped cream.

Each dish was small, but toward the end of the feast, as Dylan brought out a bowl of homemade ice cream, Alice had to wave her hands in surrender. "Please, no more. It tastes too good. But if I don't stop, I'll explode…"

Fleur smiled. "He's good, right?"

Edie said, "Hey, Dylan, tell them about your plans."

"Dreams," Dylan said, shrugging it off. "Right now, my job is making food for Gretchen."

He clearly didn't intend to tell them more. Alice thought of seeing him climb the back fence to the Pemberley's property. Could Dylan somehow have something to do with Conway's murder at the haunted house?

It seemed unlikely. He had an alibi. He would've been working the night of the murder. Plus, if tonight's visitation by Conway's ghost was part of the killer's plans, then Dylan could never have made it to the haunted house, staged the apparition, and then returned to the diner in time to make food for Edie and Fleur.

And another thing: What motive could he possibly have?

Still, he had been snooping around the inn.

Sometimes, Alice reflected, *the best approach is directness.*

"I saw you last night, you know?" Alice told him. "You were sneaking around the Pemberley Inn's backyard."

He stared at her, and for a moment, she thought he'd deny it. Then he nodded and sighed. "Yeah, that was me."

"What were you doing there?"

Ona added, "And how did you manage to outrun us? It seemed like you were teleporting from one end of my backyard to another."

"I'm fast on my feet," he said with a shrug.

"Tell them," Edie said.

He gave her a skeptical look.

"Tell them about your dreams," she added.

Dylan addressed Alice and Ona. "All right. I will. You know the Woodlander Bar, right?"

"Of course," Alice said. "We love Thor's bar."

Ona added, "I built the bar—the tiny house is one of mine."

"I know," Dylan said. "And I love the Woodlander Bar, too. See, I don't want to be Gretchen's chef forever. I've tried changing the menu. But she's not interested—she just wants to chase easy money. And that means copying whatever's on the What the Dickens Diner menu."

Alice and Ona exchanged looks. So Becca's complaint had been valid: Gretchen's strategy was to copy and undercut her rival.

"Then out of the blue, Gretchen told me she had big plans," he continued. "She was going to open a classy restaurant in an old house—a fancy place for serious foodies. I don't know if it was just a story she told me. A carrot she could dangle in front of me, you know?"

He sighed.

"See, my dream is to open my own place. It doesn't have to be big. In fact, I'd like something small, like the Woodlander Bar, where the focus is on the food I care about—and that hopefully others would care about, too."

"Oh, we'd care," Ona said. She took another hunk of bread and dipped it in her ramekin with garlicky oil and chewed it with obvious enjoyment. "We already do."

Dylan smiled and gave a nod, acknowledging the compliment. "So I was looking around at the tiny houses you've made, thinking about what kind might suit my business." He looked around at the diner. "If I ever get out of this place…"

He returned to his work in the kitchen, concocting more dishes for his guests to sample. For a while, Alice, Ona, Edie, and Fleur talked about how amazing it would be for Blithedale to have a restaurant like the one Dylan wanted to open—a place with modern comfort food. Ona was clearly pleased that Dylan admired her tiny houses. Any hard feelings about his trespassing were gone. Alice thought of Becca, and knew that their friend would be as eager to support a new restaurant in town, especially if it was housed in one of Ona's tiny houses.

Dylan brought out more dishes. Edie and Fleur talked to

him about the food, and how he'd made it. But Alice and Ona turned back to the main topic on their minds: Stewart Conway's murder.

Ona said, "So, what does it mean that Conway's ghost wanted us to know he was talking to Becca?"

"It means the killer wants us to know," Alice said. "Us and Chief Jimbo. It was a little too convenient that Jimbo turned up when he did. I bet the killer invited him."

"Another anonymous call?"

Alice nodded. Chief Jimbo had been fooled by anonymous calls before.

She said, "But I don't believe for a minute we saw a ghost."

"Another Dr. Fantasma illusion?" Ona gave that some thought. "You think Duane turning up was a coincidence? I mean, after we heard what we were meant to hear—'my little dove'—then the performance was interrupted."

Dylan was serving Edie and Fleur another set of dishes, but now turned to Alice and Ona. "'My little dove'?" he said. "I've heard that before. Stewart Conway said it."

"Wait—what?" Alice gaped at him.

For a second, she tried to figure out how Dylan had heard Conway's ghost talk.

Not the ghost, silly. Conway when he was alive.

"Where did you hear that?"

He shrugged. "Grown people can do whatever they like. It was none of my business."

"What grown people?"

"Gretchen and Stewart Conway, of course. He hung around the diner the first night he was in town, and then picked up Gretchen before closing time. They made no secret of it—or at least they weren't good at keeping it quiet. Conway wasn't exactly subtle. He was always sweet talking Gretchen. Always calling her that nickname—'my little dove.'"

Alice and Ona exchanged looks.

"Conway moved fast, huh?" Ona said. "He'd been in town for a day and he got involved with Gretchen?"

"Yeah, but it didn't last. A few days after I first saw them together—think it was Tuesday—I went out back with a bag of trash. Gretchen was standing by Conway's car. His window was open, and she leaned in and yelled at him."

"What did she say?"

"Something about staying away from her if she knew what was good for him. She was pretty angry." He shrugged. "I didn't hang around to see what happened. As I said, it was none of my business."

He went back to work.

Alice turned to Ona. "This changes everything. If Gretchen was Conway's 'little dove,' then his plea might not have been for Becca."

"Sounds like they had an affair and it didn't end happily."

"Yeah, but did it end in murder?"

CHAPTER 16

a lice and Ona left the others at the diner and headed back to the Pemberley Inn.

Main Street was dark, and all the storefronts, with their locked doors and shuttered windows, looked asleep. Alice would be glad to join them.

And a few minutes later, she did. She settled into her canopy bed in the Colonel Brandon Suite. Her mind was a swirl of thoughts: a confusing formula that involved Becca, Stewart Conway, Gretchen Tusk, and Duane Rooker. But the rich meal and the long, exhausting day bore down on her. It felt as if the bed softened, yielding to the weight of her tiredness, and she sank deeper and deeper into the mattress.

Wakefulness slammed into her. It felt only an instant after she'd closed her eyes. Now she stared into the darkness, her heart galloping in her chest.

What was that sound?

There it was again. A creaking of floorboards, a footfall outside her door, then the creak of the stairs.

She turned over in bed and checked the time.

It was 2:13 am.

She sat up. "Ona?" she whispered.

The creaking ceased outside, as if whoever was passing had heard and stopped.

Alice's heart sped up. If it had been Ona, she would've answered at once.

So, if it wasn't Ona, who was that outside her door?

She slipped out of bed. The room was cool, the frigid night air seeping through the old walls. The temperature outside must've dropped.

She tiptoed toward the door and put her hand on the icy doorknob. Slowly, she turned the lock, careful to muffle the inevitable click.

Her bare legs prickled with the cold.

She listened. Silence.

She yanked open the door.

A flash of white. A spectral figure flying up the stairs.

But if it was a ghost, it was an unusual one: Its feet thumped the stairs all the way to the landing above.

Alice chased the ghost up the stairs, grabbing the banister and pulling herself up three steps at a time.

Alice reached the final landing and looked around.

What the—?

The landing was empty. She rushed to the door to the far left. The door to the attic. But it was locked and bolted—on the outside.

She spun around. At the other end of the landing was a nook with a pedestal holding a potted plant. Behind it was nothing but dark wood paneling. But the space was too small to hide in without being seen.

Where did the ghost go?

She drifted back to the stairs, trying to make sense of the disappearance. She glanced over the railing and, looking down, caught sight of someone on the stairs below.

The ghostly figure in white.

"Hey," she said.

The figure bolted, flying down the stairs three-four steps at a time, making a racket.

Alice set off in pursuit. She ran down the stairs and almost tripped and went tumbling down, stopping herself by grabbing hold of the bannister. Then she continued down to the bottom more carefully.

No sign of the ghostly figure in the reception.

She wandered through the inn, first looking in the lounge. It was dark. She checked the French doors to the back. Locked. From there, she made her way into the kitchen, and found nothing. She opened the door to the pantry, in case the ghost was hiding inside. Empty.

"Ghost," she muttered to herself, letting out a little snort for her own benefit. "If that was a ghost, I'm a unicorn."

Still, she couldn't make sense of how the ghost had run up the stairs to the attic landing, vanished, then reappeared down below. It reminded her of Dylan's appearance in the backyard among the tiny houses. He'd seemed to appear and disappear, too, and for a while there she'd imagined him to be a ghost.

There was a connection between Dylan's visit and tonight's visitation, but he'd given the impression that he'd just been browsing for tiny houses, and alone. Did he tell the truth?

She considered waking Ona, but thought it could wait until the morning. Something strange was going on at the Pemberley Inn. But Alice's gut told her the ghost wasn't dangerous—deadly ghosts didn't make up beds and put out coffee and brownies for guests.

Then the question was…what kind of ghost did?

CHAPTER 17

The next morning, Alice told Ona about her late-night encounter, and they both went upstairs to look for signs of an intruder.

"The crazy thing is that the attic door is locked," Alice said, showing Ona the bolted door. "There's no way up. So how did the ghost elude me and then reappear halfway down the stairs?"

"I have an idea," Ona said. "Come with me."

She led Alice to the nook with the potted plant. Reaching past the pedestal, she pulled at something in the shadows—a handle maybe—and the back paneling folded up, like an accordion, sliding aside.

Alice let out a yelp of surprise.

Ona grinned. "This isn't the only secret passage in the inn."

She inched sideways past the potted plant and slid through the secret passageway in the nook. Alice did the same, careful not to knock over the plant.

The secret door led to a dark shaft. The air, heavy with

dust, tickled Alice's throat. A ladder rose toward the ceiling. Ona climbed the ladder, and Alice followed.

Reaching the top, Ona shoved at the ceiling and it swung upward, smacking down on the floor above. A trapdoor. Following Ona, Alice climbed the last rungs and then heaved herself up onto the dusty floorboards of the attic.

The slanting roof made the edges of the attic cramped. But the middle was roomy—or would've been, if there hadn't been so much old stuff: an antique, Narnia-like wardrobe; a rack full of theatrical costumes, including one for Peter Pan and another for Dracula; and boxes and suitcases and huge trash bags filled with shoes. A pair of skis lay across the top of a low bookshelf, which was filled with old hardbacks—including what looked to Alice like a complete set of the Harvard Classics.

"There's a lot of junk," Ona said. "Some of it from Old Mayor Townsend's time. I haven't spent much time up here since refurbishing the inn. Cleaning out all the stuff is on my to do list. But it's not a priority."

Alice gazed around at the collection of objects, and as she swung her attention back to Ona, her friend gave her a long, probing look.

"What?"

Ona reached into her pocket and pulled out an envelope. Alice recognized it as the one she'd left in the register downstairs.

"I found the money you left me."

"It's your money," Alice said quickly, anticipating Ona's refusal. "It's only fair I pay rent."

Ona held out the envelope. "We've talked about this before. I can't take your money."

"Look, Ona. I've given this a lot of thought. You want me to stay at the inn. I want to stay, too. But you're giving away one of your best rooms for free. If I'm going to stay long term, which I want to, then I need to contribute. No, no, hold on. Let me finish. It's not about being independent from you. It's about being a good friend and supporting the longevity of the inn."

Ona looked at her. "That was a fine speech. Did you practice it beforehand?" She sighed. "All right, you've got a point. But here's mine: You've paid the going rate for the Colonel Brandon Suite, and that's nuts. You're staying long term. So the price has to be adjusted."

She reached inside the envelope and pulled out several twenties.

"This is more reasonable."

Alice took the bills and glanced at them. "A good compromise."

Ona held out her arms, and they embraced. Alice was relieved that they'd come to an agreement that worked for both of them. It genuinely felt like they could put this behind them now.

As she hugged Ona, she looked over her shoulder.

"Hey, Ona, ghosts don't leave footprints, do they?"

They stepped apart. Alice crouched down and pointed out a footprint in the dust alongside the old wardrobe.

Ona opened its doors.

"More junk," she said, closing the doors again.

"Wait a minute."

Alice pulled open the doors again. Balled up inside were two sleeping bags. She lifted one up. Behind it was a shopping bag with cans of coke and cups of instant noodles.

Alice and Ona looked at each other.

"Provisions," Alice said.

"When I was a kid, ghosts didn't eat this kind of junk."

"Guess these are modern ghosts."

"Not one," Ona said. "But two."

"That's how the ghost could appear in two places within

such a short time. It was two ghosts. One fled through the secret passage. The other went downstairs."

Ona said, "Mystery solved."

"Almost. We still don't know who these ghosts are—or what they're doing skulking about the inn at night."

CHAPTER 18

*A*t the diner, Mayor MacDonald, in his dapper white suit, slapped a hand on the table.

"Enough, Jimbo," he told the chief of police. "Not another word about ghosts and ghouls and goblins."

Alice, who was helping Susan with the morning rush, approached the booth the two men sat in. She offered coffee refills as an excuse to eavesdrop. As she leaned over the table, pouring coffee into their cups, Chief Jimbo crossed his arms and leaned back.

"I saw what I saw," he said, a mulish expression on his face. "It's my duty to report the truth."

"Leave the sensational news to the *Blithedale Record*. It's your duty to uphold the law, maintain order, and get to the bottom of who killed Conway. Spreading stories about ghosts isn't helping."

"Actually, it is helping. Conway's ghost provided an important clue. He was clearly talking to his killer. He called her 'my little dove,' which is what he called Becca."

Alice cut in, "He also called Gretchen that. They apparently had an affair."

Chief Jimbo blinked. Then pouted. "Yeah, but Gretchen wasn't caught with the murder weapon in her hand. I don't like it anymore than you, but this only makes matters worse for Becca."

He drained his cup of coffee and got to his feet, and donned his cap. His paperback lay on the table—*The Police Chief Companion: 21 Days to Killing It On the Job*—and he picked it up.

Alice said, "But the fact that Gretchen had an affair with Conway—doesn't that change things?"

Chief Jimbo tapped the front of his paperback. "According to this, evidence speaks volumes, hearsay not so much."

Words failed her. She watched Chief Jimbo walk out of the diner. Then turned to Mayor MacDonald, who shook his head.

She said, "Just when I think he's getting better…"

"He's worse than ever. He came into the diner this morning jabbering about Conway's ghost at the old house. I was sitting right here, having a pleasant conversation with a couple of potential buyers. When they heard about the murder and the ghost, they got cold feet—they couldn't get into their car and hit the road fast enough. All thanks to our bumbling chief of police." He shook his head. "Now I have to go looking for another buyer."

"Is Peyton in a rush to sell?"

"I think she'd like to put this behind her, yes. But selling the old house wasn't her idea."

"It wasn't?"

"No, that was one of the reasons Conway came to Blithedale. To sell."

"But Dr. Fantasma—"

"Dr. Fantasma rents Conway's properties for his shows. And that's bad news for him. Because Conway wasn't just selling the property in Blithedale. He'd been visiting every haunted house property he owned and talking to realtors. He planned to sell each and every one of them."

"If Conway sold them all, what would happen to Dr. Fantasma's show?"

Mayor MacDonald shrugged. "Either he'd have to find new locations—or he'd go bust."

Alice headed back to the counter to help Susan with breakfast orders. She considered what the mayor had told her. Could Conway's plans to sell have put Dr. Fantasma's entire business in jeopardy? And if so, didn't that give him a good reason to kill Conway?

Across the diner, she spotted Dr. Fantasma and his crew. Duane Rooker looked as mean and surly as ever.

But Alice soon got busy delivering food.

At the counter, Susan handed her five breakfast plates with pancakes, eggs, and bacon and three with the yoghurt and granola special. It was for two tables occupied by the party of eight staying at the Pemberley Inn.

Alice delivered the food, served them coffee, and chatted a little, mentioning that her bookstore would open later if they wanted reading material. They were thrilled by the idea and promised to stop in later.

From across the diner, Dr. Fantasma called for the check.

Susan sidled up to Alice and nudged her.

"Do you mind dealing with Dracula over there? I've had enough of his tricks and his bloodsucking." She gestured toward Dr. Fantasma. "And Alice, tell him to use your pen when he signs the check. Got it?"

"Uh, sure thing."

That was an odd request. Who cared what pen the customer used to sign the credit card receipt? But Dr. Fantasma probably had a pen that squirted ink, or something like that.

She took the check from Susan, got out her own ballpoint pen, and headed over to Dr. Fantasma's booth.

Duane glared at her. Holly smiled and gave her a little wave.

"Good morning, Alice of Wonderland," Dr. Fantasma said. "We'd like to pay for this sumptuous meal."

She handed him the check and then the pen, saying, "Sign right here."

"With pleasure."

He reached inside his cloak and produced a fountain pen and signed the check, leaving a tip.

A big tip.

"Wow, thank you," Alice said.

She waited for the pen trick. But nothing happened.

Dr. Fantasma smiled. OK, so he was quirky, but he did act like an old-school gentleman. Hardly a "bloodsucker."

Other customers demanded her attention, and by the time she met Susan at the counter again, she'd decided that it was hard to imagine the gray-haired gentleman being a killer —or hurting anyone, for that matter.

"Dr. Fantasma was no problem at all," Alice said. "And he added a big tip."

Susan shook her head. "You let him use his pen, didn't you?"

She opened the check holder and showed it to Alice.

The bill came to $30 without the tip. But the numbers Dr. Fantasma had scrawled with his fountain pen—as well as his signature—were hardly legible, and even as Alice stared at the ink, it faded, and faded, and faded. Until it was nearly gone.

She looked up at Susan, who sighed.

"See, told you he'd play tricks on you."

"Vanishing ink."

"Awful, isn't it?"

But Alice was thinking it was great. Because it meant Becca's blank note from Stewart Conway—the one asking her to meet him at the haunted house—wasn't a mystery, after all. The message had been written in vanishing ink.

She glanced over toward Dr. Fantasma's booth. It was empty.

"Yup," Susan said. "He's left without paying again. He seems to think it's funny. But it's theft—plain and simple theft—and I ought to report it as a crime."

But Alice was wondering whether theft was Dr. Fantasma's only crime.

CHAPTER 19

True to their word, the party of eight from the inn visited Wonderland Books later that morning. After their hearty breakfast at the diner, they'd gone hiking in the woods, they told Alice, and they were heads over heels in love with Blithedale's natural surroundings.

They ignored the Halloween displays and instead browsed for books about nature and hiking, and before long, Alice had sold copies of *Walden, Wild, All Creatures Great and Small*, and *Finding the Mother Tree*. One of them couldn't seem to settle on the right book for her, though, and Alice tried to help.

"I'm not even sure what I'm looking for."

"Something about nature?"

"Yeah, I guess so…"

"A special mood?"

The woman gave it some thought. Then said, "When I was a kid, my family and I used to go to this cabin in New Hampshire. It wasn't fancy. In fact, it was pretty basic. There was a lake and woods. Nothing to do but explore and read and play board games. One year, I went with my grandma.

Just her and me." She stared off into the middle distance, a wistful look on her face. "It's hard to explain, but something about that summer changed my relationship to my grandma."

Alice nodded. "I have a book recommendation for you."

She led the woman to one of the shelves and took down Tove Jansson's *The Summer Book*. She said, "This is about a six-year-old girl who spends the summer with her grandmother on an island in Finland. The simplicity of the place, and something about the close quarters, deepens their relationship in a beautiful way."

She handed the woman the slim book.

"Hmm…not exactly a Halloween book," the woman said.

She opened the book and read the first page and smiled.

"Oh, but I'm going to like this."

The group paid for their books and headed out again, leaving the tiny house quiet after their chatter and laughter.

Alice felt good. What was more gratifying than recommending the right book to another person? It was like sharing a bit of love with them—a magical way to connect with a friend or a stranger.

The only other feeling as gratifying was solving a mystery.

But she resisted the urge to consider the mystery. She needed time with her books. She spent the next hour restocking shelves and wiling away the time, reading the first sentences of novels and promising herself she'd read or reread this or that one.

Mid-morning, Alice closed the bookstore, and she and Ona visited Becca at the police station.

Alice was surprised to see that Becca's cell had been transformed. The few amenities she'd started out with had mushroomed. The bed—now softened with a thick mattress —was heaped with blankets and pillows. There was also a giant beanbag, a poster on the wall of Niagara Falls, a lava lamp, a clothing rack with a variety of Becca's outfits, a foot-bath, and a flat screen TV, replacing the old set that Jimbo had first installed.

Becca sat in a deck chair watching the TV when they came to visit.

Chief Jimbo unlocked the cell door and promised to bring lunch soon.

"Chief Jimbo's worried I won't be comfortable," Becca said with a smile, "so he keeps bringing more and more things into my cell. Soon, I won't be able to fit."

Alice stared at all the objects crammed into the small cell. There was a boom box for music, a bunch of board games, a stack of magazines, even a box full of Legos—apparently a reflection of one of Chief Jimbo's own hobbies.

"You have better amenities than I have back at the inn," Ona said.

"But how are you?" Alice asked.

Becca shrugged. "Bored—and worried about my diner—but I'm doing all right. Hotel Jimbo takes care of its guests."

Alice was relieved to see that Becca was doing well. But every day her friend spent locked up was one day too much. And when she asked Becca about how likely it seemed Chief Jimbo would release her, Becca grimaced.

"That fool says his book has a step-by-step process for investigating crimes, and when he pencils in all the evidence against me, it tells him there's no doubt I killed Conway."

"But he told me he doesn't believe you killed him."

"Oh, he tells me that, too," Becca said with a sigh. "He doesn't believe I could do it. But he trusts his book more than his own gut."

Ona slapped a hand to her forehead. "What a fool."

Alice shook her head. "Honestly, I can't make sense of him. Usually, he wants problems to go away. Why wouldn't he simply release you, Becca, and go back to the police station being as quiet as usual?"

"Beats me," she said.

"Ona, we've got to find out what Conway's ghost really was. And who's behind it."

"Agreed." Ona checked the time. "But right now I need to go help Susan with the lunch rush. If there is one. Half the town seems to be hanging out at Gretchen's diner."

Becca flinched. "Gretchen."

Alice said, "Yes, Gretchen. We need to talk to her."

Chief Jimbo came back and locked the cell, Ona headed off to the diner, and Alice returned to Wonderland Books. As she approached the red door to the tiny house, she noticed a brown paper bag on the steps.

What was this?

She unlocked the door to the store and stepped inside, putting the paper bag on the counter. Once she'd flipped the sign to "Come In We're Open," she opened the bag.

Inside was a card. It said, "The Darn Good Diner."

She tensed. Why was Gretchen leaving bags on her doorstep?

She flipped the card over and saw a message scrawled there:

Enjoy your lunch!
Dylan

Inside the bag was a takeout container of soup and a sandwich wrapped up in butcher's paper. Alice unwrapped the sandwich. Smoked salmon on a bed of arugula topped with a poached egg and a dijon dressing on toasted sourdough. It smelled heavenly. So did the soup. White beans, crushed tomatoes, baby spinach, topped with parmesan cheese.

It was another example of Dylan's talent in the kitchen.

Super nice of him, she thought. Then stopped herself mid-spoonful of soup. *Yeah, super nice.*

Why was he being so nice?

Not that people needed a reason to be nice. Alice enjoyed being nice—it was its own reward. But Dylan had been standoffish at first. Could this be the influence of Edie and Fleur? Probably.

She ate her lunch, relishing each bite.

After lunch, she cleaned up and continued her work at the bookstore.

It was quiet. Not good for business, but she enjoyed the solitude. Then, late in the afternoon, two familiar customers turned up: Todd Townsend, the lanky owner of the local newspaper, the *Blithedale Record*, and Beau Bowers, owner of the Blithedale Theater.

Seconds after ducking under the lintel, Todd leaned against the counter. He asked Alice about the murder case, fishing for details for his news site. But Beau was busy searching the shelves for a book, slipping books out and then shoving them back in, as he chewed his lower lip.

Finally, he let out a triumphant, "Yes—here it is."

He brought a book to the counter that Alice had forgotten she'd ordered a while back. It was intended for teens. A beginner's guide to magic tricks.

"I'd like to add a magic show to the theater's line-up. And I thought I'd better read up on what some of the standard tricks are."

Todd said, "And this has nothing to do with your love of magic?"

Beau blushed. "Oh, all right. I admit it. I love magic tricks.

Always have. In fact, Dr. Fantasma did this thing with a salt shaker the other day…"

Alice groaned. "Made the salt disappear and then reappear?"

"That's right."

"There was a pepper illusion, too."

"You mean Pepper's ghost?"

"I meant with the pepper shaker. But what's Pepper's ghost?"

Beau opened the book he was buying and flipped through, then turned it so she could see the spread. A 19th century illustration showed a theater stage with a space below it where a projector cast light on a ghostly figure, which was then reflected in an angled pane of glass on stage, making it appear as if there was a transparent, spectral figure on stage.

"That's Pepper's ghost," Beau said. "The Blithedale Theater used it back in the vaudeville days. It's an old illusion trick that allows you to create a kind of apparition—it looks as if a translucent ghost is hovering in front of you."

"Wait a minute." Alice studied the illustration and read the accompanying text. "Could anyone set this up?"

Beau nodded. "Sure. With the right materials—a pane of glass, a light source, and the right controlled conditions. Like in a theater."

"Or in an old mansion at night," Alice muttered to herself.

CHAPTER 20

That night, after helping at the diner, Alice and Ona returned to the old Victorian house in the woods.

Alice explained how the Pepper's ghost illusion worked. But despite the rational explanation, the old house still looked creepy.

As they climbed the steps to the front porch, Ona said, "It looks no less haunted tonight."

"I'm not worried about ghosts."

Ona glanced over her shoulder. "Glad to see Duane's car isn't here? Me, too."

Alice tried the front door. It was locked this time. She took that as a good sign. The first time had been a setup. This time, hopefully, no one knew they were coming.

The porch wrapped all the way around the house. Whereas the front windows all had curtains, the back ones were boarded up. There was a door, though. Ona grabbed the door handle and turned it, and its rusty mechanism grated—making Alice's shoulders tense—but opened easily enough.

"So much for locked doors," Ona said.

Alice gazed out at the dark trees. Their leaves shushed in the wind, an ominous sound under the best of circumstances. She tried not to make too much of it—or the feeling that the house itself seemed to watch them warily as they stepped over its threshold.

Inside was a kitchen. It was dusty. Appliances had once stood against the walls, but they'd been torn out, leaving gaping holes. There an old door with a padlock, but otherwise the place was empty. Ona led the way into a corridor. At the end, a door stood open, and that brought them into the entrance foyer with the massive staircase.

Ona stopped.

"What?" Alice whispered.

"Just listening."

Alice did the same. They stood listening for a while.

"Nothing," Ona said.

"Nothing," Alice agreed.

But it didn't make her feel any less creeped out. Would creaking floorboards have made her more confident? Of course not. But if there'd been stomping and someone had been playing music and there'd been voices, she could've told herself people—real-life, flesh-and-blood humans—were gathered for ordinary purposes. Sometimes silence was worse.

Her first step on the stairs set off a deep groan, and her whole spine seized up.

On second thought, silence is just fine.

She moved up the stairs, treading with the caution of someone on dangerously thin ice. Maybe because the house was so still, she and Ona kept whispering and trying to make as little noise as possible. Once, she set off another groan that rippled into a series of creaks, and Ona gave her a sharp look.

"Sorry," Alice muttered.

Ona was much better at moving up the old staircase without making too much noise.

Not fair, Alice thought to herself. *She's had years of practice in that old inn of hers.*

They reached the first landing, and both of them stopped and looked upward. Alice half-expected to see Conway's ghost again. If he'd repeated his ghostly plea the other night, why wouldn't he do so again?

Because he wasn't a ghost. Just an illusion. And illusions won't scare me off.

Alice took a deep breath, grabbed the banister, and took another step upward. Ona followed close behind. The closer they came to the top landing, the more Alice expected some ghostly figure to come floating out of the wall. Knowing rationally that something couldn't be a ghost didn't seem to stop one's imagination from anticipating the worst.

But no ghost appeared.

Alice and Ona stood in the spot they'd seen Conway's ghost.

"Well…?" Ona whispered.

"Well."

Alice examined the area. Musty drapes framed a window, which had been boarded up to keep out the light. No doubt for the benefit of the haunted house experience. But apart from the curtains and carpeting and wainscoting, the landing was bare. She checked the door to the west wing. It was open.

Inside was darkness and the vague outlines of a room.

"This room was part of the haunted house experience," she whispered to Ona. "What if this door was open when we stood down below—we wouldn't have noticed, would we?"

"Don't think so, no."

She stooped by the entrance to the room. There was a double socket in the wall.

"Someone could've set up a projector here. And a glass partition over there…"

"Glass? Wouldn't that be difficult to set up?"

Alice stood up. "Plexiglass, then. Beau's magic book suggested that worked just as well."

"Makes sense. But the Pepper's ghost you described was done live. We saw Conway after he died. Could the killer have used a projector to show a recording?"

Alice nodded. "The Princess Leia effect, some people call it. I bet the killer recorded Conway before he died—maybe the moment before his death—and that's what we saw played back as a projection on the stairs." She gestured toward the other door. "The killer could also have set up over there. After all, it was in the east wing that Conway was killed."

"And where Becca was framed."

"Let's take a look."

Alice led the way to the door across the landing. She was about to turn the handle when she heard a sound from within. A shuffling or sliding, as if something were being dragged across the floor.

She turned to Ona, who nodded. She opened the door.

It was dark inside. This was the corridor they'd run down the night they'd found Becca standing over Conway's dead body.

Gretchen had been standing there, too, Alice thought.

She tiptoed down the corridor, glad to have Ona at her back. She couldn't imagine doing this on her own. She'd grown up alone, her aunt and uncle often moving, making it difficult to meet—and keep—friends. Her childhood had taught her self-reliance. Coming to Blithedale, she'd at first insisted on doing things on her own, relying on her lifelong independence. But Ona and Becca had shown her there was a better way—a way to get things done with friends by your side. It was a lesson she especially appreciated now. Who would want to be self-reliant in a haunted house?

At the end of the corridor, the door to the room Conway had died in stood open. Alice slowed down and peeked inside. As before, it was dark. The walls, draped in heavy curtains from top to bottom, seemed to ripple—and maybe they did. Had something disturbed the curtains?

Something or someone...

She stepped inside. Ona followed, their shoulders touching. Alice resisted the urge to grab her friend's hand, worried that the unexpected touch might frighten her. But then she felt Ona's hand wrap around hers—she must've felt the same way—and their mingled warmth spread up Alice's arm. She felt safer, stronger.

Good thing, too. Because in front of them, where Conway's dead body had lain, something materialized out of the dark. A milky white form shimmered and flickered into being. A creature with sagging, corrupted flesh on its face and a long, torn robe fluttering at its ankles floated above the floor.

The ghoul hissed.

Ona's grip tightened on Alice's hand.

"Not," Alice said through clenched teeth, "a ghost."

She stepped forward, dragging Ona with her, and raised her free hand and struck at the ghoul. Her hand passed right through the apparition. She looked around in the room, and a flicker of light caught her attention.

"There—to the right!"

She let go of Ona and rushed toward the darkness. She barreled into an invisible wall—the impact a hard smack—and she staggered back. But her weight knocked the wall over. Light flashed across the pane as it toppled over and slammed to the floor.

Plexiglass, Alice thought, and in that moment, a figure rushed out of the dark, cutting across a beam of light.

The ghoul screamed with very human rage as it slammed into Alice.

Alice spun around herself, losing her balance, and fell to the floor.

Ona swung at the ghoul, but it ducked, then vanished into the folds of the black curtains. Its footsteps thundered down a corridor, diminishing as it got further and further away.

"You all right?" Ona asked, bending over Alice.

"I'm fine. Get the ghoul!"

Ona rushed after the attacker. But she struggled to find the exit from the room, wrestling with the heavy drapes, shoving them this way and that. Finally, she found a door and threw it open and rushed after the ghoul.

Alice's shoulder ached where the ghoul had struck her, but nothing was broken, and she got to her feet and stumbled after her friend.

The dark corridor beyond the drapes was empty. Alice moved along it, opening doors and peering inside at empty floorboards and—where there was furniture—creepy shapes covered in sheets.

Ona reappeared at the end of the corridor.

She shook her head. "It's gone."

Alice found a light switch. A dim lamp flickered to life overheard. Ona regarded it with a wry look. "Now, why didn't we think of that earlier?"

"Because we'd convinced ourselves we were in a haunted house, and you don't turn on the lights in a haunted house. You creep along in the dark and whisper, and expect the next thing you see to be a ghost."

"Sounds just about stupid enough to be true. It also means this: The mansion has electricity. Which fits with your idea of a projector being used."

"Come on," Alice said. "Let's look at the scene of the crime again."

Behind the black curtains, they found a light switch and turned it on.

Because the back of the room had been dark, it had seemed to Alice that the space was half its size and square. In fact, the room bent sharply—two squares arranged in a dogleg—and there was a large recess in one section of a wall. The Plexiglass, which now lay on the floor, had split the room in two. Beyond it stood the light projector, its beam of light aimed at where the Plexiglas had stood.

"Pepper's ghost," Alice said. "This was all a theatrical illusion."

"And that ghoul—"

"—was a living, breathing human being."

"You mean a living, breathing murderer."

CHAPTER 21

*A*lice called Chief Jimbo, and together the three of them turned on every light in the mansion and, from the kitchen to the top stairs, searched every nook and cranny. In the west wing, they found theatrical equipment. Robotics to make the skeletons move. Speakers to emit ghoulish voices. And even projectors set up to cast creepy light under doors, on ceilings, against walls.

But what they didn't find was a killer.

Back in the room where the ghoul had appeared, Chief Jimbo agreed the Plexiglass was important evidence. But he couldn't say it changed the overall picture.

"Even if someone's been playing tricks on us, Becca was caught with the murder weapon in her hand. She followed Conway into this room. She was right behind him."

"A few seconds is all it would take to stab a man," Alice insisted.

"Record him," Chief Jimbo said. "And then stab him?"

Alice bit her lip. He had a point. How could Conway's killer have threatened him, recorded his plea, then killed him just in time for Becca to appear in the room? It made no sense.

"Maybe the recording was from earlier…"

"Sorry," Chief Jimbo said. "I can't release Becca. What would the citizens of Blithedale say if I did?"

"Uh, thank you?" Ona suggested.

Chief Jimbo shook his head. "Gretchen Tusk is popular, and her testimony points to Becca being the killer. If I ignore that, imagine what people will say at the diner."

"The diner?"

"The Darn Good Diner."

Alice gritted her teeth. Chief Jimbo was calling Gretchen's place "the diner"? If this continued for much longer, the What the Dickens diner would go out of business.

"That woman, Gretchen Tusk, is bad news," she said. "We'd all be better off if she'd never come to Blithedale."

"Or if she'd move on," Ona said, nodding.

Chief Jimbo looked uncomfortable. "I prefer Becca's food, but her prices…"

"Don't talk to me about prices," Alice snapped. "There's something suspicious about that woman."

"You think she did all this illusion stuff?"

"I don't know," Alice said, gazing around at the black drapes along the walls, which reminded her of a theater. A very morbid theater. "There is one person who's an expert at illusions and magic tricks. And he's definitely keeping secrets."

"Dr. Fantasma," Ona said.

"Dr. Fantasma?" Chief Jimbo seemed outraged. "But I grew up on his magic shows. He's an institution. Why would he hurt Conway?"

Alice thought of what Mayor MacDonald had told her. If Conway had planned to sell all his haunted houses, and it meant Dr. Fantasma would go out of business, how far would the old man go to save his own neck?

She nudged Ona. Ona didn't need her to say a thing. She nodded, understanding perfectly well what they had to do.

She leaned close. "But first…"

"First?"

Ona yawned. "I need some sleep."

CHAPTER 22

*T*he next morning, Alice and Ona intended to help Susan out at the diner, but Susan told them not to bother.

"Unless a miracle happens, we won't have enough customers to make my job difficult."

She gestured at the tables and booths, most of them empty this morning. The Darn Good Diner had a new breakfast special on—twice the amount of food at half the price. And a surprise Halloween treat for each customer. Even the most loyal customers had been lured over there, too curious to resist.

Alice and Ona ate breakfast in morose silence. Of course, people could choose to eat where they wanted. They'd probably just say that Becca ought to cut her prices. The truth was that she already had. But dropping them to the depths of the Darn Good Diner would be financial suicide.

Alice finished her yoghurt with granola and drained her cup of coffee. "Let's go."

In the parking lot, they got into Ona's pickup. As Ona revved the engine and they pulled out onto Main Street,

Alice considered what they knew about Dr. Fantasma. He'd been coming to Blithedale for a couple of decades. Everyone knew him and his haunted houses. People had grown up on his shows. Her own memories from her childhood were positive—even magical.

Driving into the woods, she asked Ona what she knew about him.

"I didn't grow up in Blithedale, so I have a more adult perspective. He's fine, I guess. Fun. Entertaining. But there's something—" She shrugged. "—I don't know, sad about him."

"Sad?"

"Yeah, maybe it's the signs of a man in decline that make me think that. When I first came to Blithedale, his shows were extravagant. They used to use the entire haunted house for the show. He traveled with a dozen actors and several technicians. Now, he's down to a skeleton crew." She smirked. "Pardon the pun."

"What happened?"

"Guess we have to ask him that. But I can guess. Haunted house experiences have changed over the years. They used to be all Nancy Drew, Hardy Boys, Scooby Doo, and these days they're like stepping into your own personal nightmare. Like you're an expendable extra on the set of *Saw*."

Alice nodded, recognizing the development. "Haunted houses went from fun to frightening to terrifying. They changed. But Dr. Fantasma didn't."

They approached the Blithedale campgrounds, and Ona pulled into the gravel parking lot by the office. A bearded, burly man in a flannel shirt and jeans came out sipping coffee from a camper's tin cup.

"Morning, ladies," he said.

"We're here to visit Dr. Fantasma."

"Back there. You can't miss him. He and his crew are the only guests—since the temperature dropped, any campers in regular tents have pulled up stakes and found other places to stay."

Three campers stood parked on one of the little designated lots. One of them was garishly painted, including with a giant, cartoonish portrait of Dr. Fantasma himself.

"I bet I know which camper is his," Ona said.

But on their way there, they passed a nondescript camper. Its door stood ajar and voices drifted out. Coming closer, Alice recognized the voices as belonging to Duane and Holly.

Duane said, "There's got to be another way…"

"You're not listening to me, Duane. My mom needs me here in Blithedale. I've got to stay."

"I'm starting my own business. Haunted house experiences like we do now, but modern. Up to date. And I need talented people, Holly. I need you."

She sighed. "You told me that already. And I appreciate it. I really do, but I—"

"A good job. Free from Dr. Fantasma. Free from the Conways of this world."

"In my new life in Blithedale, I'll be free from Fantasma, anyway. And Conway—"

"Conway's dead." Duane let out a huff of exasperation. "You still don't understand, do you? I'll do anything for you, Holly. Anything." Then he lowered his voice. "You need money? I can lend you money."

"No, thanks."

"You need a friend. Doing this on your own, it's madness, it's—"

"Stop, Duane. Just stop. No more. You've done enough."

There was a long silence. Then the camper creaked and Duane appeared in the doorway. When he saw Alice and Ona standing nearby, he frowned.

Alice kept walking, hoping it looked as if they'd simply been passing by.

"Morning, Duane," Ona said.

Duane's response was a threatening glare.

Alice hurried to Dr. Fantasma's camper and knocked on the door.

"Enter ye, enter ye."

Alice opened the door and stepped up into the camper. Ona followed and shut the door behind them.

The camper's cramped quarters were made more constricted by costumes on hangers dangling from dozens of hooks set into the walls. A plastic skeleton sat on a counter, one bony arm slung over an aquarium. Inside the aquarium, eyeballs floated in murky water. Dr. Fantasma sat in a tiny booth, a book open in front of him and, next to it, a steaming cup of tea.

He smiled broadly and gestured for them to join him.

"What a delightful surprise. I certainly did not expect visitors today. Come, come. Can I offer tea? Coffee?"

"Nothing, thanks."

Alice slid into the booth. Ona got comfortable next to her. Or at least as comfortable as either of them could. They were so crammed into the tiny space that everyone's knees jostled each other and Alice pressed up against Ona's hip.

Dr. Fantasma regarded them.

"I'm a magician, but no fortune teller. Yet I can guess why you're here, and it's not because of my magic tricks."

"Actually, Dr. Fantasma, it is about your magic tricks."

"Oh?" His eyes lit up, and he rubbed his hands together. "Do tell. Nothing brings me greater joy."

Alice and Ona exchanged glances, and Ona nodded at Alice. They'd talked about this ahead of time. They needed to present the facts and see how Dr. Fantasma responded.

"Last night," Alice began, "we discovered how the ghoul that Mrs. Oriel saw appeared, and how the same person created what we were meant to believe was Stewart Conway's ghost."

"Go on."

"Pepper's ghost."

Dr. Fantasma reached out and grasped Alice's hand. With a smile, he whispered, "You worked it out."

"Worked it out?"

"My little clue."

"Wait, you mean the pepper shaker trick—that was a clue?"

"Of course it was. In fact, I worried I was being far too obvious."

Alice sighed. "Why didn't you just tell me?"

"Tell you?" Dr. Fantasma retracted his hand as he chuckled. "Where's the fun in that? Besides, we were in a very public place. Someone might've heard."

Obviously, he meant the killer. It annoyed Alice that she'd had to deal with Dr. Fantasma's cryptic riddles, but at least they were getting somewhere now.

"Did you use Pepper's ghost in the haunted house show?"

"We've used it many times in the past, but we didn't this year."

"Why not?"

"Duane was against it. He argued for a more modern approach. He wanted more video projectors. 'Put away the Plexiglas,' he told me, 'and give me money to buy projectors.' So I did."

"Is Duane in charge of setting up?"

Dr. Fantasma nodded. "He oversees the equipment, the setup, and even much of the conceptual work. He's got a knack for all these newfangled gadgets. I find it hard to keep up. Though I still have a bit of my old star power left, I've reduced my involvement in recent years."

The way he said it didn't come across as bragging. It came across as sad—exactly what Ona had described.

Dr. Fantasma added, "Thank goodness for Duane. He planned everything this year. Including how we'd run a full show with such reduced staff."

"He decided the east wing should be shut down?"

"Certainly, and it was a wise decision."

"So he knows every shortcut in the mansion."

"Of course. It's his job."

Dr. Fantasma's eyes widened. "Good God, you're not implying…?"

"I overheard Duane threatening Stewart Conway outside the Pemberley Inn. Duane had access to vanishing ink, and could've written the note to Becca, claiming it was from Conway. Meanwhile, he could've falsified an invitation from Becca to Conway—or found some other way to lure him to the mansion. Knowing the old mansion so well, he could've led Mrs. Oriel through the room until she came to the murder scene to witness the Pepper's ghost scene."

"But why would he?" Dr. Fantasma shook his head. "What would Duane get out of killing Stewart Conway?"

Alice had considered this. "Conway was going to sell all the haunted houses. It would've destroyed your business. Duane must've found out. His career would be in jeopardy—his career and yours."

And Holly's, she considered. *The conversation they'd just overheard suggested Duane had feelings for the young woman. Duane himself had said he'd do anything for her. Did that include murder?*

Dr. Fantasma shook his head. "But Duane already knew about Conway selling."

"He knew?"

"I told him."

"You knew, too?"

Dr. Fantasma took a sip of his tea. He had rings under his eyes. He looked old—much older than Alice had at first thought.

"I've known for a while. Stewart told me. In fact, he enjoyed telling me, no doubt thinking it would shock me. And I was upset at first. But with time, I also realized that I was relieved. It gave me an excuse to plan my retirement." He let out a long sigh. "I'm too old for this racket. Kids don't want phantasmagoria. They don't want the Grand Guignol. They want such horrifying experiences that they come away with PTSD. I can't give them that, and I don't want to."

"But why didn't Conway simply rent out to a more modern haunted house outfit?"

"He wanted to sell every haunted house property he owned. He wanted out of the landlord business altogether. I suppose he needed money."

"Did he already have buyers lined up?"

"Yes, he talked about having a buyer lined up—a lover who was going to set up her business in the mansion. But I got the sense Conway wasn't averse to making promises he couldn't keep, especially to women."

Alice and Ona exchanged glances. Dylan had mentioned something about Gretchen's big plans to open a serious restaurant in an old house. What if that was the old Victorian mansion Conway planned to sell? And what if Conway promised Gretchen that she could get the house for a cheap price—and it turned out to be a lie?

Dylan had said Gretchen had been furious at Conway. How furious? Angry enough to kill?

CHAPTER 23

*A*lice spent the rest of the day at Wonderland Books. Business was brisk, but she took a break before lunch, closing for 15 minutes to visit the Darn Good Diner.

She wanted to talk to Gretchen. But Gretchen wasn't at the diner. Dylan said he didn't know where she was. Alice returned in the afternoon on another 15-minute break. This time, she spotted Gretchen behind the counter, but when Alice tried to strike up a conversation, Gretchen was anything but friendly.

"Can't you see I'm busy?" she snapped.

Alice gave up and returned to her bookstore.

She had a few more customers in the afternoon, including Todd, who pretended to want to buy a book for his "bedtime reading," but really wanted to ask her more questions about the murder investigation. She revealed what she and Ona had found at the mansion, but didn't talk about Gretchen.

Todd said, "Sounds like we should be taking a closer look at Dr. Fantasma and his crew. I actually went to talk to Duane Rooker. He chased me off. I had the feeling he would've given me a black eye, or worse, if I didn't clear out fast."

"He's a tough guy."

"I talked to a journalist friend in Philly who said Dr. Fantasma did a haunted house experience in Pennsylvania, and Rooker got into some trouble."

"What kind of trouble?"

"Bar brawl. Broke a guy's jaw. Spent the night in jail."

"And?"

"And they dropped the charges."

Todd bought the Library of America's edition of Edgar Allan Poe's *Poetry and Tales* for his bedtime reading. After he left, Alice wondered what to make of the information he'd shared.

Duane had a temper. He'd gotten into fights. He'd threatened Conway. Putting those details together with the fact that he had the know-how to pull off the Pepper's ghost illusion, he fit the bill as the killer. But she'd prefer to cast Gretchen in the role.

You just want her to be the killer because of the diner, she told herself.

It was true. Alice was biased. But that didn't mean Gretchen wasn't the killer.

With these thoughts on her mind, she closed up the bookstore and headed back to the inn. She'd left her key in the reception and grabbed it. She could see from the rack of keys that the other guests on the second floor must be out.

She headed to the stairs, which were dim, the stairwell submerged in darkness. She flipped the light switch, but it didn't seem to work.

Dead light bulb? Gotta tell Ona about that...

As she climbed the stairs, she whispered a hello to each of the framed portraits of Jane Austen characters that lined the wall: Elinor Dashwood, Emma Woodhouse, Frank Churchill, Jane Bennet, even the wicked George Wickham.

She'd almost reached the landing when she heard a sound above her and looked up the stairwell. A flash of white by the top banister. And then something came hurtling down toward her.

She stepped back as a flower pot struck the stairs in front of her with a great crash. Shards of pottery flew across the carpeted steps. Dirt cascaded down and hit her sneakers. The poor plant settled on one of the steps, its scraggly roots exposed.

She was about to continue up when she heard footsteps. Ona appeared at the bottom of the stairs.

"What happened? Are you all right?"

She flipped the light switch. Click, click, click. Nothing happened, of course.

"Lights out," Alice said. "And someone threw a potted plant at me from above. I think it was our ghost from the attic."

"Hold on."

Ona drew out her phone, turned on the flashlight, and hurried up the stairs. Alice made to continue upward, but Ona grasped her by the shoulder.

"Stop." She held Alice in place. "Look."

In the light of her flashlight, Alice saw something shimmer. Just above the top step, a wire ran across the landing.

Alice bent down. "What is that?"

"Let's find out."

Ona reached out. She crooked a finger and snagged the wire. She pulled. The wire, taught, resisted her pull—and then there was a snap. Something flew through the air. Thunk!

Alice looked up. A crossbow bolt vibrated in the wall, embedded in a portrait of Lady Catherine de Bourgh.

"If I'd kept on going…" Alice muttered. "If I hadn't stopped because of that potted plant exploding at my feet…"

"You'd have an arrow in your head."

Alice gazed upward. "Then the ghost…"

"The ghost saved your life."

CHAPTER 24

*L*ater, when Chief Jimbo was dismantling the crossbow mechanism with the tripwire, Alice and Ona searched the upstairs, opening the secret passage and examining the attic. But except for the potted plant, now missing from the pedestal by the secret passage, everything looked the same as before. They found no sign of a ghost. It had vanished again.

Coming back to the landing, Chief Jimbo hailed them from afar.

"Come look at this."

He held up the crossbow and turned it over. Underneath, it said, "Musselwhite Theatrical Supplies, Inc."

Ona let out a low whistle. "So now even theater props can kill—why bother going to a gun store?"

"It's been modified," Chief Jimbo said. "Look. This bolt is a metal rod that's been sharpened, probably with a metal saw."

"Homemade," Ona said.

Chief Jimbo nodded. "Homemade."

Alice took the crossbow from Chief Jimbo and examined

it. The whole setup was a pretty elaborate way to kill some-one. Crossbow. Home-whittled bolt. Tripwire. A gun would've been easier. Maybe the killer didn't have a gun—or didn't like them. Or maybe the killer didn't want to be caught holding a murder weapon.

Either way, the killer had targeted her directly.

She said, "We're getting close to the truth. The killer's getting worried."

She held up the crossbow. Where the trigger met the wood, a single strand of hair stuck out. She drew Chief Jimbo's attention to it, and he grabbed an evidence bag and a pair of tweezers.

"It's in chapter twelve of my book. It says I should always carry bags and tweezers."

He bagged the hair and held it up to the light.

Alice and Ona crowded around to take a look.

It was a single, curly hair. Bright red.

"Only one person has hair that red," Ona said. "Gretchen."

Alice surveyed the landing again. "But how could Gretchen set something like this up?" She filled Chief Jimbo in on what Dr. Fantasma had told them about Conway and Duane—including his expertise in gadgetry. "If Duane Rooker had curly, red hair, I would've said we'd made a breakthrough. He's got the knowledge to rig up a trap like this. But Gretchen?"

Ona nodded. "Yeah, it's not your typical diner owner's choice of murder weapon."

Chief Jimbo pocketed the bag with the hair. "But then she didn't always own a diner."

"What do you mean?" Alice asked.

"I interviewed her after Conway's death, and she told me. She ran a salon before she opened the Darn Good Diner. And before that she ran a pet store. She was the manager of a sporting goods store for a while, too."

Chief Jimbo beamed, obviously proud of his modest accomplishment.

Alice said, "Sporting goods store? Would they sell a crossbow at a store like that?"

"Maybe," Ona said. "But remember, this one's from a theatrical supplies company."

"Right. So unless she worked with theater props…"

"Which she didn't…" Chief Jimbo said. He grabbed the wire, the crossbow, and the stand that had held it, and started to descend the stairs. As he walked down, he added, thinking out loud, "Though maybe they'd carry similar stuff at a magic store…"

Alice went to the banister and leaned over. "What was that you said, Jimbo?"

He looked up. "Gretchen. Before she worked in sporting goods, she worked at her parents' store in the city. It was a magic shop."

CHAPTER 25

he next morning, Alice risked looking like she'd stabbed Becca in the back by turning up at the Darn Good Diner for breakfast. She made a point of sitting at the counter where Gretchen couldn't avoid her.

"What'll it be?" Gretchen asked, and Alice couldn't help but stare at her unnaturally bright red curls. "Come on, I've got other customers waiting."

"Coffee. A bran muffin."

"That's it?"

"That—and a question."

"This isn't *Dear Abby*." She poured Alice a cup of coffee. "Go ask someone else."

Alice leaned across the counter and dropped her voice to a whisper. "I know about you and Conway."

Gretchen stared at her. Then she leaned close.

"And so what?" she whispered. "Think I care? You don't know anything."

She pushed back from the counter and walked away. A moment later, she came back and dropped a brown bag with a bran muffin in it on the counter.

"Here's your muffin," she said, "to go."

"Listen, Gretchen—"

"Go."

Alice took the hint, grabbed her muffin, and headed out. She wandered down Main Street and headed straight for the What the Dickens Diner to get a proper breakfast.

What did her encounter with Gretchen tell her? That she was rude and hostile to Becca and her friends. But nothing told Alice with any certainty that Gretchen had murdered Stewart Conway and then rigged up a crossbow to fire at Blithedale's bookseller.

She'd have to find another opportunity to corner Gretchen. At work, the woman was in her element. Maybe she could catch her after hours instead. But where?

As she grabbed the door to the What the Dickens Diner, she saw a poster in the window.

Tonight: Live Halloween music at the Woodlander Bar! The Pointed Firs will be whipping up a fine blend of spooky bluegrass for your enjoyment. Come one, come all!

That was it. If the Pointed Firs were playing at the Woodlander Bar, half of Blithedale would turn up. Maybe Gretchen would, too. It was worth a shot.

Besides, Alice thought as she stepped into the warm, cozy diner, *Who can say no to a Pointed Firs concert?*

Apparently, very few people could, because by the time Alice and Ona showed up at the Woodlander Bar that night, the parking lot was jam-packed and every table was claimed.

The bar looked as magical as ever. The tiny house—built by Ona for Thor—sat off a road running through the Blithedale Woods. A gravelly area accommodated tables and hurricane lanterns, while the bar itself was inside the tiny house, too small to accommodate many guests.

Fortunately, the wind had calmed. The air was crisp and cool, but not as frigid as before. Plus, Thor had set up patio heaters next to the tables, their warm glow keeping the worst of the chill from the guests.

Alice spotted the party of eight from the inn, all crammed into one table. Dr. Fantasma sat at another table with Duane and Holly. Even looking at Duane gave Alice the chills. But she turned her attention away from him, looking for her real target: Gretchen.

Mayor MacDonald hobnobbed with the Oriels and Andrea Connor of Bonsai & Pie, and they waved at Ona and Alice. Peyton Conway occupied the chair next to the mayor. Beyond them, at another table, sat Dylan with the purple-haired girls, Edie and Fleur. They waved, too.

There was a space in the middle of the tables for the band, and Althea Strong and her bandmates were tuning their instruments: guitar, banjo, upright bass, and fiddle.

While Ona looked for a place to sit, Alice headed inside to get drinks. Behind the bar, the owner, Thor, was busy mixing cocktails. He had long blonde hair and a handsome face that could've landed him a career in fashion or movies. He gave Alice a big smile.

"Half the town is here tonight," Alice said.

"A good night. Soon, the cold weather will slow business to a trickle. Once the snow comes, outdoor serving will be limited to the hardiest people."

"I hear your mulled wine is irresistible."

"It warms you all the way to your toes. You want one now?"

"I'll wait for Christmas. But how about a glass of red wine? Make it two."

"You got it."

As Thor filled the glasses, someone came to stand next to Alice at the bar. She turned and saw that it was Peyton

Conway. They greeted each other and made small talk about the bar.

Then Alice said, "Guess you're stuck in Blithedale until you can sell that house."

"Actually, I found a buyer." Peyton shrugged. "It's less money than I'd hoped to sell it for. Much less. But it feels right."

"Feels right?"

"A young woman is moving to Blithedale to be close to her aging mother, and she wants to start a business. The old Victorian is perfect for her needs."

"You aren't talking about Holly, are you?"

"That's right. She's carrying on Dr. Fantasma's work, but with a permanent home here in town."

Thor handed Alice her glasses of wine.

Alice turned back to Peyton. "A year-round haunted house?"

"As I understand it, she won't limit herself to haunted house experiences. Thank God. I can't stand those things."

"Not a Halloween fan?"

Peyton shook her head decisively. "No, thank you. I was glad to learn that Holly plans to do Christmas and Easter and murder mystery evenings, and all kinds of immersive experiences. She's got ideas, that young woman."

A voice said, "Ideas are a dime a dozen."

Gretchen leaned against the bar. She laughed. Even her laugh sounded slurred, like she'd had a few drinks already.

"Ideas are a dime a dozen, and young women are two a penny..."

She waved Thor down and pointed at an empty glass, then raised two fingers and added another two. Thor nodded, brought out a bottle of bourbon, and poured, and poured, and poured. He nearly filled Gretchen's glass.

Peyton made a face, got her drink from Thor, and gave

Alice a goodbye nod. Then left the bar. But Alice didn't allow Gretchen's apparent drunken behavior to scare her off.

"What are you staring at?" Gretchen said, taking a drink.

"I was wondering," Alice said, "whether you paid a visit to my room yesterday."

"Sweetheart, even if I preferred women, you'd never be my type."

"I was talking about the cute trick with the tripwire and crossbow."

Gretchen took a big gulp of bourbon and swallowed. "Cute tricks? I'm all about cute tricks. But I can't remember when I last handled a crossbow. Uh, let me think…that's right, never. I've never handled a crossbow."

"We found your hair on it."

Gretchen stared at her. Then burst out laughing. She laughed and laughed, wiping tears from her eyes. "Oh, that's good. That's very good."

"What are you talking about?"

"Poor little Alice doesn't know…"

Sharp barbs of anger pricked Alice's insides. She was losing her patience with this woman. "Well, why don't you tell me, then?"

Gretchen leaned close, her boozy breath hot on Alice's face.

"I know things," Gretchen said, glancing around to make sure no one was listening. "I know things that would shock you. I know what really happened at that haunted house. I know who killed Conway."

Her words sent a jolt of electricity through Alice's body.

"You said Becca did. But you saw the actual killer, didn't you?"

"I didn't know what I saw until later. Then I put two and two together."

Alice grabbed Gretchen by the arm. "Who did it? Tell me."

"I'll tell you," Gretchen said, removing Alice's hand, "when you pay me."

"Pay you?"

"A grand oughta do it."

"Wait, are you asking for $1,000?"

"You catch on quick, sweetheart."

Alice stared at Gretchen, aware that her jaw had dropped.

Outside, the bluegrass band launched into their first tune, and people hooted and clapped.

But Alice's attention was too focused on Gretchen to pay much attention. She couldn't believe the woman's brazen money-grabbing. Here was an opportunity to clear Becca's name—and Gretchen demanded payment. It was blackmail. But if she knew who killed Conway, how much was that information worth? If it got Becca out of jail, it was invaluable.

"I don't have that kind of money on me," she said.

"But you can get it." Gretchen downed her glass of bourbon and wiped her mouth with the back of her hand. "Meet me at midnight behind the diner. Bring the money in cash. Then I'll tell you everything."

She set down her glass on the bar and turned—and ran right into Duane Rooker. Gretchen's eyes widened. She scurried around him and muttered something under her breath, her bravura suddenly gone. She gave a backward glance before hurrying out of the tiny house.

Duane gave Alice a hard stare.

"What?" he said. "You got something to say to me?"

Alice shook her head. She had nothing to say. But she hoped Gretchen had lots to say tonight.

CHAPTER 26

"*I* love this," Ona said from behind the wheel of her pickup as they pulled into the parking lot of the Darn Good Diner. "Meeting at midnight. Handing over a bag full of money. I love it."

Alice looked over at her. "You do?"

"No. I was being sarcastic. But either I'm too tired to do sarcasm or you're too tired to hear it."

She pulled the pickup into a parking spot and cut the engine.

"It's a terrible idea," she said. "Harebrained."

"But we need to know. If Gretchen saw the killer, and she can tell us, then what choice do we have?"

"No choice. But I don't have to like it, do I?"

Alice couldn't disagree with that. She didn't like it, either. The brown paper bag she clutched in her hands contained $1,000, which they'd cobbled together from their own accounts, plus with help from Mayor MacDonald.

He hadn't wanted to know what they needed it for.

"Obviously, it's something to do with the murder investigation," he'd said. "Which makes it important. So, tell me later."

Afterward, Alice reflected that you couldn't always anticipate how people would act in a crisis. Mayor MacDonald had his flaws, but when his friends or his beloved town were in trouble, he'd do anything to help.

Ona was the same way. And so was Becca. With any luck, Gretchen could provide the evidence they needed to free Becca—and stop the killer. Tonight, they might end this murder investigation once and for all.

They got out of the pickup.

The Darn Good Diner was dark. Apparently, Dylan hadn't stayed late tonight. Maybe he was still with Edie and Fleur at the Woodlander Bar. Alice and Ona moved around the building to the back. The parking lot wrapped around the diner, leading them to the rows of trash cans, and beyond that, the wall of dark trees. The Blithedale Woods were always there, wherever you looked, the old trees as much a part of town as the storefronts along Main Street.

They rounded the building. A car stood parked sideways in front of the trash cans. Gretchen's car, no doubt.

Ona put out a hand, stopping Alice.

"What's that?"

Alice craned her neck. It looked as if someone was lying on the other side of the car.

Alice and Ona exchanged glances, then both broke into a run. Coming around the side of the car, Alice saw the body. It was Gretchen. She was lying between the car and the trash cans. Face down. Her back a bloody mess. A knife protruded from the back.

"Stabbed," Ona said and put a hand on Gretchen's neck. "No pulse. But she's warm."

Alice looked around. The killer must've been here moments before they arrived. How else could a midnight rendezvous turn into a crime scene before Alice and Ona even arrived?

Then she saw something wrapped around the hilt of the knife. A piece of paper fastened with a rubber band. The outside of the paper said, "Read me."

Alice pried the paper off, but the rubber band was tricky, and she had to grasp the knife before getting it off. She unfolded the message. In the dim light, the message was hard to read. Squinting, Alice read it aloud:

Meet me at 11:30 pm instead. Same place.
I've got the cash.

Alice

As Alice read the message, she squinted harder. Was the parking lot getting darker? It was as if the light was fading. No, the light wasn't fading. But the message was. She got out her phone, turned on her flashlight, and caught the last clear outlines of letters as they were vanishing.

Vanishing ink again.

Gretchen was dead. The truth about the killer gone. She'd been a fool to agree to Gretchen's plans—she should've got the truth out of her at the bar. She should've called Chief Jimbo and somehow, with the threat of police involvement, made Gretchen talk. Instead, she'd gone along with her plan to exchange money and information at midnight, and now things couldn't possibly get any worse.

A car pulled into the parking lot. A door slammed. Chief Jimbo rounded Gretchen's car, his belt jiggling with its gun and flashlight. When he saw the body, he sucked in a breath. He rushed forward and bent over Alice, reading the note.

"What've you done?" he asked, horrified.

"I didn't—this wasn't me—I—"

Ona said, "Come on, Jimbo, you don't honestly think we'd—"

"Look at your hands," Chief Jimbo said.

Alice looked down. There was blood on her hands. She must've smeared her hands with blood when she'd removed the note from the knife.

Oh, no, the knife...

Her fingerprints were on the hilt of the knife. She'd been careless. Stupid. But surely Chief Jimbo would understand…

"It's not what it looks like…" she said.

Chief Jimbo stepped back. He dug out his paperback from his back copy and flipped through the pages, biting his lower lip as his eyes scanned the text. Finally, he let out a sigh.

"Sorry, Alice…"

He put away the book and grabbed his handcuffs.

"Alice Hartford, you're under arrest for suspicion of murder…"

Alice groaned. Apparently, things could get worse.

CHAPTER 27

*C*hief Jimbo closed the cell door with a clank and locked it. Alice grabbed the bars. She said, "Come on, Jimbo, you know we didn't do it."

Becca and Ona stood by her side, all three of them behind bars.

Chief Jimbo, a worried look pinching his face, dug out his dog-eared paperback and flipped through the pages. He read aloud, *"Real detective work is not like the movies. Most criminals are caught at or near the scene of the crime. In 98.9 percent of cases, fingerprints on the murder weapon belong to the perp. The killer is almost always the most obvious suspect."* He put the book away. "I'm sorry, Alice and Ona, but I've got to go by the book."

Ona said, "You know that's just an expression, right? You don't literally need to follow everything that your book says."

Chief Jimbo gave her a confused look, and Ona sighed.

"What's the point of trying?" she muttered.

He said, "Deep down, I know you ladies are innocent. Trust me. I'm working on a solution to this mystery, and soon you'll all be free. I just need to reread a couple of chapters in my book before bedtime…"

Chief Jimbo wished them a goodnight and walked away, leaving the three friends alone. A moment later, the lights in the cell and down the corridor dimmed, though they didn't go out.

Distantly, she heard the front door of the police station shut. Soon, Chief Jimbo would be home, getting reading for bed, reading his trusted paperback guide to policing. Alice wasn't confident that he'd find an answer in his book to who killed Stewart Conway and Gretchen Tusk.

Meanwhile, she and her friends stood in a tiny—though comfortable—jail cell with dim lights overhead. Jimbo had put them all together, justifying it by saying it was now by far the most comfortable cell. Alice didn't disagree, and besides, she preferred to be close to Becca and Ona.

Still, this was a disaster.

"If we're stuck in here," Alice said. "Who's going to catch the killer?"

"Chief Jimbo?" Ona said. Then grimaced. "Sorry, bad joke."

Becca wrapped her arms around Alice and Ona. "We'll figure this out. After all, you didn't kill Gretchen." She cocked her head and regarded them for a moment. "You didn't, did you?"

"No," Alice said. "Of course, we didn't."

"Wanted to, at times," Ona added. "But didn't."

"So, who wanted to kill her?" Becca asked, releasing them from her embrace.

Alice sighed. She plopped down on the bed heaped with pillows and hugged her knees to her chest. She considered what had led to Gretchen's death.

She said, "At the Woodlander Bar, Gretchen hinted she knew who the killer was. But she wanted money. She called for a midnight meeting. She was careful to tell me without others hearing. But she was drunk—and overconfident—and when she was about to leave, she literally ran into Duane."

"Duane Rooker?" Ona said.

Alice nodded. "Gretchen seemed shocked to see him. Even frightened. I wonder whether Duane heard the last bit of our conversation. He knew we were meeting at midnight, even if he might not know why."

"But if he was the killer," Becca said, "then he wouldn't need to know why, would he?"

"What makes you say that?"

"Well, Gretchen immediately jumped at the chance to make money off her knowledge. She must've known about the killer for a while. Let's assume she put together the puzzle shortly after I was arrested. Maybe after the appearance of Stewart's so-called ghost. Then why did she wait so long to offer to tell you?"

Alice shrugged. "She didn't know I was interested?"

"Of course she knew. The whole town knows you and Ona want to get me out of jail."

"Becca, you're right," Ona said. "Gretchen wouldn't wait, unless she had a valid reason. And Gretchen only ever had one reason for doing things."

"Money," Becca said and made a face.

Alice's mind lit up with the realization. "She was black-mailing the killer. That's why she waited. But then why turn to me for money?"

"Because the killer refused to pay?" Ona suggested. "Maybe Gretchen was asking for more money, too much, and the killer couldn't raise that kind of cash."

"Ten grand," Alice said, nodding. "That was a big amount. I bet you're right. Gretchen squeezed the killer for money, but she got greedy. She wanted more. She realized she could sell her information to another party."

"To us," Ona said. "Except someone overheard."

"Duane Rooker."

Again and again, Duane Rooker kept popping up. He threatened Conway. He was at the haunted house the night of the murder and knew his way around better than anyone else. The setup for the show and all the gadgets were his responsibility. The night Conway's ghost appeared, he turned up. And he overheard Gretchen tell Alice to meet her at midnight behind the Darn Good Diner.

Alice said, "Gretchen behaved horribly, and I wanted her to be the killer. I played right into Rooker's hands. He must've rigged up the crossbow and left a red hair to suggest Gretchen did it."

"Mean-looking Duane Rooker," Ona said, nodding. "What is it Chief Jimbo's book says? 'The killer is almost always the most obvious suspect.' Now all we need to do is stop him before he gets away with murder."

"Which we can't do," Alice said, "from within a prison cell."

She let out a long sigh.

Then the lights cut out. The cell plunged into pitch blackness. Alice slipped off the bed and bumped into someone. Ona muttered a curse. Someone stepped on her foot and Alice let out a yelp. Becca whispered, "Sorry. No room in here. What happened? Who turned off the lights?"

"Shh…" Ona again. "Someone's out there."

An icy chill ran down Alice's neck.

Duane Rooker, she thought. *He's come to finish us off, and we're sitting ducks.*

The sound of footsteps. She craned her neck, trying to see who was coming down the corridor. The footsteps—shuffling, dragging feet—came closer and closer. And then her heart leaped into her throat when she saw the ghostly white figure floating toward them. No, not just one. Two ghosts drifting down the corridor.

"Ona," Alice hissed.

"I see them."

"It's the Pemberley ghosts."

CHAPTER 28

*O*ne of the ghosts said, "It's too dark. I can't see where I put the keys."

The other, seeming to wrestle with itself, brought out a cell phone and turned on the flashlight. A bright light bloomed and Alice threw a hand up to protect her eyes.

"Ah," the first ghost told her buddy. "That's better."

Keys? Cell phones? Then Alice heard keys in the lock and a loud click. With a clank, the door opened. The second ghost shone the light at Alice.

Alice said, "Hey, point that thing someplace else, will you?"

"Oh, sorry, Alice."

Alice squinted. She knew that voice.

"Fleur?"

The ghost whipped off her hood. Underneath was Fleur, purple hair and all, grinning. Edie removed her hood, too. They were wearing white, hooded bathrobes. In the light, they didn't look ghostly at all.

Alice said, "You're the ghosts?"

"We can explain," Fleur said. "See—"

"Later," Edie said, cutting her off. "We've got to get you all out of here before Chief Jimbo finds out. We didn't know how to disable the security system, so we cut the power. It's probably on a backup generator. I bet Chief Jimbo already got notified that there was a break-in."

Alice didn't need to be told twice. Nor did Becca and Ona. The three friends filed out of the cell and followed Edie and Fleur down the corridor.

They emerged into the police department's main space, with its two desks, only one of which was in use. From here, Edie and Fleur led them to a back door.

Outside, the night air was icy cold, and Alice, who wasn't wearing a coat, hugged herself.

Edie said, "The car's over there."

A beat-up Honda stood parked a little way off in the parking lot. They ran over to the car, and as they approached, the inside lit up and the driver's door swung open.

Dylan grinned from within. "You made it."

"We're not home free yet," Edie said. "Everyone pile in."

Alice, Becca, and Ona did as they were told. Alice jumped into the backseat first. Becca and Ona followed, with Fleur squeezing in at the end. Edie got in the passenger seat in the front as Dylan turned the ignition.

But the escape wasn't a dramatic wheel-spinning race through town. Dylan put the car in drive and rolled down the street at just under the speed limit, as calmly as if they were taking a scenic tour. At this rate, it would take them ages to put the police department far behind them. Alice bit her lip.

"No point in drawing attention to ourselves," Dylan said, maybe sensing his passengers' worry. "And look, here comes Chief Jimbo."

The cruiser flew past them, its lights flashing. Alice

ducked down. Chief Jimbo rarely used the lights or the sirens, but he seemed to be getting more and more accustomed to the lights. He apparently didn't see the escaped prisoners in the getaway car. His cruiser vanished in the distance, and soon Dylan pulled up at the curb in front of the Pemberley Inn.

"Uh," Alice said. "Isn't this the first place Chief Jimbo will look for us?"

"Sure," Edie said. "But he won't find us."

They got out of the car and hurried inside. Creeping up the stairs, Edie and Fleur led them to the top landing. Then through the secret passage behind the pedestal—now free of its broken potted plant. But instead of leading them up to the attic, Fleur knocked the wall across from the ladder and the panel shifted. She pulled it aside, revealing darkness beyond.

"Follow me," she said.

CHAPTER 29

"*H*uh," Ona said. "Will you look at that? Another secret passage."

Fleur led the way. A ladder led down a shaft to a landing. Then to another ladder, which also reached a landing, and onward to another ladder stretching downward. In the dark shaft, Alice lost the sense of how far they were descending.

Finally, Fleur jumped off the rungs and landed at the bottom. She pushed open a door and light spilled onto the bottom of the ladder. Alice, reaching the floor, followed the young woman into a cellar.

It must once have been a root or coal cellar. Its walls seemed to have been carved out of the rock that the inn was built on, and to one side sat a massive boulder. The air was cold and damp, but Fleur stooped at an old wood-burning stove in a corner and threw bits of wood inside, then started a fire.

"Where are we?" Ona asked, gazing around her with wonder.

"We're in the other cellar," Fleur said. "There's the basement you already know, and then there's this one, bricked up behind the basement."

Edie produced several old straight-backed chairs in the Shaker style. They all sat down around the wood-burning stove, and Alice rubbed her hands and held them out to the heat.

Then she turned to Edie, Fleur, and Dylan, and said, "All right. The first order of business is a big thank you. That was an amazing rescue. I've never been busted out of jail before."

Becca and Ona jumped in, heaping praises on the three rescuers, and Edie and Fleur, grinning, exchanged glances, and Dylan gave a modest shrug.

"Now, why don't you tell us everything," Alice said.

"Everything?" Edie asked.

"Everything. Starting with why you've been playing ghosts at the inn."

Fleur frowned. "We feel terrible about that."

"Yeah, awful," Edie said, nodding.

"We were staying at the camping grounds."

"But then the temperature dropped, and it just got too cold."

Alice thought for a moment. She remembered learning that Edie and Fleur were staying at the camping grounds, but then when she and Ona went to see Dr. Fantasma, they were told the guests staying in tents had moved on. She hadn't considered that it would include Edie and Fleur.

Fleur continued: "We couldn't afford to pay rent. But we were going to die of cold, so one night, getting desperate, we snuck into the inn. First, we thought we could stay in a tiny house, but they were too cold, too. Then we considered the lounge, but the inn was busy, and someone would definitely see us."

"But we got lucky and found the attic," Edie said. "We went up through the regular door the first night. And while we were exploring the space, we found the trapdoor to the secret passage. Before we found the panel that led to the landing by the attic entrance, we found the door to the shaft leading down here. We re-bolted the main door to the attic and started using the secret door instead, sleeping upstairs in the attic at night, where it's warmer, and then hiding down here during the day, where it's pretty cold."

Ona laughed. "Amazing. You know the inn better than I do. But why the white bath robes?"

"They're nice and warm," Edie said.

"Plus, we knew we risked being spotted," Fleur said. "We also knew we could hide quickly. The bathrobes hid our identities. Caused confusion. We never thought people would think we were ghosts."

Alice jumped in. "Wait a minute. You two were in the backyard with Dylan the night Ona and I chased him, weren't you?"

Edie and Fleur nodded, looking embarrassed.

Edie said, "We helped him get into the backyard. When you came out, we tried to draw you away."

"Which is why it seemed Dylan could move so fast," Alice said. "There were three of you. That was also how the Pemberley Inn ghost could vanish upstairs and appear downstairs a moment later—the two of you were running in opposite directions, making me think I was going crazy."

"Are you mad at us?" Fleur asked, a nervous look on her face.

"Mad?" Ona said. "You saved my butt when that party of eight turned up. That was you, wasn't it—making up the rooms and putting out refreshments for them?"

Edie and Fleur nodded. "The least we could do. We tried to help as much as possible, cleaning and tidying, setting up for guests, and finding books around town that you could use at your bookstore, Alice."

"And it was you who saved my life, too," Alice said. "You threw a potted plant at me to stop me from stumbling into the tripwire that would've left a crossbow bolt in my side."

"We heard something," Edie said. "It must've been the killer setting up the trap. We almost stumbled into it ourselves. Then waited around for you to come home to warn you. We didn't want to fiddle with the trap, in case we left our fingerprints all over it."

Alice muttered, "You're smarter about fingerprints than I am…"

"But why?" Ona said, lifting her hands in a gesture of confusion. "Why go through all this elaborate charade to keep your presence a secret?"

"We couldn't pay rent," Edie said.

Ona said, "But you could've asked for help. Why didn't you?"

Edie and Fleur exchanged looks.

Edie said, "We don't have anything to offer."

"Clearly, you have a lot to offer," Ona said. "You've just described how busy you've been helping guests and foiling booby traps. All for free."

"Not for free," Fleur insisted. "We've been living in your house. We wanted to pay you in some way."

Alice glanced over at Dylan. "Was this why you sent me that delicious lunch?"

He shrugged. "It felt like the right thing to do. You let me off the hook for breaking into the backyard that night. Plus, you and Ona have been so generous to Edie and Fleur. I wish I could offer them a place to stay, but I rent a room in someone's house—that's all I've got right now."

"So, you see," Edie said, "we only wanted to do what was right."

Alice and Ona looked at each other and laughed. Finally, the mystery of the friendly Pemberley ghosts was solved.

Edie and Fleur's reason to keep their presence a secret felt so recognizable to Alice—it was the old self-reliance rearing its head. Recently, she herself would've gone to great lengths to prove her worth rather than ask for help.

Now, Ona said, "Edie, Fleur. You two need a place to stay. I have a giant mansion. Until you have money to pay rent, you can stay with me—you got it? If it makes you feel better, you can help with chores. But no need to be creeping around in bathrobes. Got it?"

Edie and Fleur nodded. "Thank you," they said in unison.

"Well, that's one mystery wrapped up," Ona said.

"Now we need to stop the person who killed Stewart and Gretchen," Becca added.

Edie and Fleur exchanged looks. Alice leaned forward in her chair. "You two know something?"

Edie turned to Dylan. "Tell them what you told us about Gretchen's business."

Dylan rubbed his chin for a moment. Then said, "The thing with Gretchen was that money was tight. Always tight. She thought she could drop her prices and squeeze out the competition—"

"That would be me," Becca said.

"That's right. Once you were out of business, she was going to raise her prices. But she couldn't afford it. She was reckless. She burned through her savings to keep her prices so low. And after she paid suppliers, there was no money left over to pay me. When I threatened to leave, she dangled a carrot—told me we were going to move to a bigger, better location, and I could finally create the dishes I wanted to create."

"She was moving out of Blithedale?" Becca asked.

Dylan shook his head. "No, she was going to open a luxury restaurant here in Blithedale. I told her it sounded like bull. If she couldn't pay me, she couldn't afford to open a luxury restaurant. She insisted she had a friend who was getting her a killer deal on the real estate for the restaurant."

Alice looked at Ona, then at Becca.

Becca nodded. "Stewart. When he was trying to sweet talk me at the diner, he hinted he had a property that might interest me. Maybe I should open a second restaurant? Or maybe I wanted to live in a beautiful, old Victorian?"

"Conway must've promised Gretchen the old Victorian that he was using for the haunted house," Alice said. "He would've promised it to you, too, Becca, if you hadn't dismissed his advances. Go on, Dylan. What else?"

"Well, Gretchen and Conway broke off their affair. I told you about that already. After that, she said the deal was off. No luxury restaurant. I said if I didn't get my wages, I'd walk. Then—it must've been the day after Conway died—she suddenly hands me a big wad of bills. All the money she owes me."

"Did she tell you how she got it?"

Dylan shook his head. "But she said there was more coming."

Alice, Becca, and Ona nodded at each other.

"Blackmail money," Ona said.

Alice rested her elbows on her knees and, with steepled fingers at her chin, gave some thought to everything they'd learned so far. It was time to bring the killer out into the open. She told the others what she wanted to do. Edie and Fleur called it dangerous. Dylan said he knew about food, not about catching killers. But Becca and Ona nodded and agreed—they had to strike now.

Alice's phone was still at the police department, so she borrowed Dylan's. She made a call to the Blithedale camping grounds, waking the poor owner and apologizing profusely, saying it was an emergency. She got the number she needed. Then dialed it.

"Duane?" she said when she got him on the line. "Yes, I know what time it is. Yes, I have a good reason for calling. I know the truth about Stewart Conway and Gretchen Tusk's deaths. We need to talk. Meet me at the haunted house in two hours."

She hung up.

"What did he say?" Ona asked.

"He said he'd be there."

Ona stood up. "That means we don't have much time to prepare."

Everyone else got to their feet.

Alice smiled. "Let's get ready for the show."

CHAPTER 30

*D*riving up to the old Victorian mansion in Ona's pickup truck, Alice was relieved to see the parking lot was empty. The pickup rumbled and bumped along the potholes as Ona steered it around the building to the back. She parked close to the porch steps.

Alice got out on the passenger side, followed by Becca. Ona got out on the driver's side, her backpack in her hand. They'd left Edie, Fleur, and Dylan behind, telling them to keep an eye on the inn.

Listening, Alice heard nothing but the rustle of leaves in the wind. She breathed deeply, the cool, clear air filling her chest. Then she climbed the steps to the kitchen door and opened it.

Inside, the run-down kitchen looked the same as before. Dusty. Abandoned. Depressing. This time, she also noticed that the old, padlocked door, presumably to a cellar, had been defaced with graffiti long ago. The paint had faded—or maybe someone had tried unsuccessfully to scrub it off—but it lent the place an even more forlorn feeling.

As she moved into the hallway and the foyer, the decorations might be more intact, but the feeling only intensified. Now that she felt no more fear of ghosts, the old Victorian mansion simply looked run down.

With Becca and Ona behind her, Alice climbed the staircase. The stairs creaked. Things seemed to go skittering behind the wainscoting. A draft tickled her neck. The higher they went, the more her stomach tensed. Any moment now, that ghoul might jump out at them. She wasn't afraid of the dead rising—but a murderer was on the loose.

The doors to the east and west wings remained closed, though, and on the top landing, she paused again and gestured for Becca and Ona to be still, too. Alice leaned close to the door to the east wing. No sounds. No sign anyone else was in the house.

"Come on," Alice whispered.

She opened the door, and the three of them crept down the dark hallway to the room where Stewart Conway had been killed.

"Back again," Becca said, surveying the black-curtained room.

"Here," Alice said. "Help me get this into place."

She dragged the Plexiglas out from behind the curtains where Chief Jimbo had left it. There were grooves in the floor, recently sawn, and the glass fit neatly into the slots. The projector was where the killer had left it.

"You got your gear?" she asked Ona.

Ona nodded and, crouching down, zipped open her backpack and pulled out the costume she'd wear: a Regency dress, plus a Halloween zombie mask. It wouldn't stand up to scrutiny, but it was the only mask they'd found at the inn, and they hoped they only needed to startle Duane.

Ona got into her dress and then moved behind the Plexiglas, joining Alice near the projector. Becca stayed on the other side.

Ona got into position and pulled on the mask.

"I'm ready," she said, her voice muffled by the rubber.

"Here we go."

Alice turned on the projector. Light spilled across Ona, and Becca let out a "huh." Then she said, "It's a good trick. Now I see Ona's ghost through the glass."

With the test a success, Alice turned off the projector. Becca hid behind a curtain. And they waited.

Alice listened to the old mansion. Apart from its by-now-familiar creaks, it was quiet. So quiet she almost thought she could hear the shushing of the leaves in the wind outside. Then, under that shushing, she heard a rumble. Distantly. Then closer. Finally, the sound drowned out the rustling leaves as it approached the house.

A car. It was loud and clear now as it entered the grounds.

The engine stopped. A door slammed. Then another.

She heard voices outside the house. Too distant and muffled to make sense of. But then one voice rose in pitch, a man's voice: "No, I won't let you." Then another voice, but less clear, too faint to hear. Then the man again: "I'll take care of this."

The front door slammed shut downstairs—it was far away, but she could hear its muffled crash through the house.

She waited. Her breathing sounded like waves crashing on a beach. Her heart grew to the volume of a gong. She tried to be still, wanting to hear.

Then she did hear. The door down the corridor opening and closing, and footsteps approaching. She turned on the projector as Duane appeared in the room.

"What the—?"

Even in the gloom, Alice could see the frown on his face. Ona made a gravelly sound in her throat, as if she were choking. It sent chills down Alice's spine.

Ona, in a ghostly voice, said, "The dead know who killed

Stewart Conway. The dead know who killed Gretchen Tusk. The dead—"

"Oh, for God's sake," Duane said, apparently unaffected. "Turn that damn thing off. You don't think I know Pepper's ghost when I see it?"

Ona's spectral image shrugged and turned around. "No luck, Alice."

Alice switched off the projector, plummeting the room into darkness. But an instant later, lights overhead glowed to life, casting a yellow sheen over them all.

Ona tore off her zombie mask. She and Alice emerged from behind the Plexiglas. Becca followed from the behind the curtains.

Alice said, "We know about Pepper's ghost, too, and how Mrs. Oriel was tricked into believing a ghoul had killed Conway. But it wasn't a ghoul that killed Conway, was it?"

"Conway got what he deserved," Duane said, facing her. "No one will miss him. It's time you left this alone. It's none of your business."

"And Gretchen Tusk—did she get what she deserved, too?"

Duane rubbed the back of his neck. "She shouldn't have— I never expected—"

"But you stabbed her, like you stabbed Stewart."

Duane stared at Alice for a while, as if considering something. Then said, "All right. I killed them. Happy?" He took a deep breath and let it out. "Conway was a creep. He manipulated women, finding their weakest spot or greatest need, and then exploiting that. And Gretchen Tusk was—"

"A blackmailer?" Alice said. "She must've seen you leave the scene of the crime. But she didn't understand who it was. Then afterward, she realized. And she decided you'd pay to keep her mouth shut."

"That's right. Let's call the cops. I'm turning myself in."

Alice barely heard him as her mind fixed on a detail. "If Mrs. Oriel saw the ghoul, and then Gretchen saw Conway on the stairs, it must mean—"

Suddenly, a missing piece slipped into place in the puzzle, and Alice understood. The thing she hadn't been able to make sense of was the timing. How did the killer confront Conway, record him (so he could appear as a ghost later), kill him, then set up Becca, given how little time passed between Conway entering the east wing and Becca following him?

Now she understood.

"He was already dead," she said. "Conway was already dead when he appeared on the stairs and led Becca into this room. But it wasn't an illusion. It was a much simpler trick. The killer put on his distinctive blue trench coat. Becca glimpsed it, thinking it must be Conway, and she followed. Gretchen caught a glimpse, too. But afterward, she must've realized something wasn't right—some detail didn't sit right with her. Maybe she saw the shoes were wrong."

Duane balled his fists. "Yeah, fine. That was me. I wore the wrong shoes. Can we go now?"

"So, then the killer did have time to record Conway in the east wing before killing him."

"Yes, I filmed him. Then I stabbed him."

"No, you didn't. For two reasons. First, you were in the west wing, keeping an eye on the room with the mist-filled glass cage. You wouldn't have had time to go to the east wing and murder Conway. Second, Conway called his killer by her nickname: 'my little dove.' The same term of endearment he'd used for Becca and Gretchen. The same term of endearment he no doubt used for every woman he tried to seduce."

"No," Duane said. "It was me. I'm telling you, it was me."

"It was never you," Alice said. "But it was someone you love. Someone you've been trying to protect."

Duane seemed to chew some invisible gristle in his

mouth. He clenched and unclenched his fists, as his face grew paler.

"You don't know," he said, his voice weak, almost a whisper. "You don't know anything."

"You're in love with her, aren't you? You'd do anything for her—even go to prison for murders you didn't commit."

Duane looked away, clenching his jaw. Something went out of him and the hardness fell away, his shoulders slumping.

Cautiously, Becca stepped up to him and put a hand on his arm. She said, "Where is she, Duane? Where is she now?"

But already Alice knew.

CHAPTER 31

*T*he padlock on the door in the kitchen—the one with the faded graffiti—turned out to be a fake. Another magic store prop. After a little fiddling, Alice got it open. Then found stone steps leading downward. It was cool and damp, the same as in the inn's old cellar.

But that's where the similarities ended.

The walls were brick. Metal shelving lined one wall. A long work table stood along another. And on every surface—from the shelves to the floor itself—sat equipment that she'd expect to see in the wings of a theater.

Projectors. Robotic arms. Oversized nets that seemed too big to catch butterflies or fish—in fact, they must've been made to snatch big animals, maybe even people.

And then there was the life-sized doll of a ghoul.

No, Alice thought. *Not a doll. A mannequin wearing a costume.*

Holly sat at the table, her back to Alice. She wore all black — the kind of outfit stage hands wore in theaters to blend into the background — but she'd accented it with a red scarf.

Maybe one of her mother's. As Alice came down the last step, she spoke without turning.

"Duane said he'd take care of it. But he doesn't have the guts. He'd sacrifice himself to keep me out of prison." She shook her head. "But he'd never do the real hard work."

"Duane knew you killed Conway."

"He guessed it."

Alice approached the table. She moved cautiously, aware that she might be walking into a trap. But Holly sat still, her hands balled up in her lap, her shoulders slumped.

On the table in front of her, among metal boxes full of wires and an alarm clock that blinked the wrong time, was a framed photograph of herself and her mother. Her mother, instantly recognizable, was many years younger—and many times healthier.

"You love her," Alice said.

"She's my mom."

Holly seemed to think that explained everything.

To Alice, it was enough. Her own mom had meant the world to her, and her death had turned everything upside down. She'd only been 9 years old, but if she'd been older and she thought she had the chance to help her, how far would she go?

"You wanted to start a new business here in Blithedale."

"I need to stay close to my mom. And I need money to pay for her treatment."

"You killed Conway because of this house?"

"He promised me the house. I couldn't pay much. He said it didn't matter. He loved me." She sounded weary, but then her voice hardened. "He lied to me. It was one of his games. I was one of his conquests, and once he had me in his bed, he forgot all about his promise."

Alice leaned against the edge of the table. So, it was never about getting money. It was about getting revenge on a man who took advantage of women for his own amusement.

"You lured him to the room upstairs. You told him it was over, and you threatened him with something. To kill him?"

Holly laughed. It was a low, bitter laugh. "Nothing like that. I threatened to tell his wife. He pleaded with me to keep quiet."

"And you recorded the whole thing, so you could use it later to project an apparition of him."

"A simple trick of the trade."

"But why get Becca involved?"

"It was either Becca or Gretchen, one of his past lovers, and I thought Becca would be easier to manipulate. Gretchen was mad at Conway and might not show up at his invitation."

"You stabbed him. Then staged an elaborate ghostly scene, drawing Mrs. Oriel into the room. Why?"

"It caused confusion. It also meant that the witnesses would be doubted. I needed one thing to seem like a delusion and another to seem like the obvious truth: Becca killed Conway."

"It was you that Becca and Gretchen saw on the stairs—you wearing Conway's blue coat. And later, overhearing that Ona and I would return to the house, you staged Conway's apparition."

Holly said, "I made a call to Chief Jimbo, so he could come and hear from Conway himself who murdered him. You were a bonus. I hoped you'd be frightened off." She made a face. "But then you came back. I was down here in the cellar and heard you. And I thought my ghoul would frighten you, but it didn't. My crossbow didn't even stop you."

"And meanwhile, Gretchen was blackmailing you."

"I couldn't afford to lose money to her. I hardly had enough to start my business and settle in Blithedale. But she kept pressing."

"She was going to sell the information to me. But she spoke too loudly and Duane overheard. He told you about our meeting, didn't he?"

She nodded. "He said he'd find a solution and made me promise not to do anything drastic. But Duane's so naïve. He thinks he can fix things with his knuckles and tough-guy routine. The only way to fix Gretchen was to silence her. Forever."

Alice sighed. "I'm sorry you think so, Holly. If you'd talked to people in Blithedale, you might've found that many here are willing to help. But the time for that has passed, hasn't it? Now, it's time for you to come with me. It's time to—"

Holly shook her head. "There's no more time."

There was something odd about how she said it. Alice cocked her head and studied the young woman. She said, "What do you mean?"

Holly gestured with her chin at the table in front of her.

"My little gadget will go off soon. Then this house will disappear, like vanishing ink, and so will all the problems within it."

Alice felt as if someone rammed a metal rod down her spine. She jerked to her feet.

"What? Is that—is that a—"

"Bomb," Holly said calmly.

The metal boxes with wires. Lots of wires. Red wire. Blue wire. Green wire. Even a red wire coiled around a black one. The digital alarm clock showed the wrong time. Except it wasn't the wrong time—with each flash, it was counting down.

Three minutes.

Alice grabbed Holly's arm. "We've got to leave."

"No." Holly shook her head. "No one leaves."

Becca. Ona. Duane. They were still upstairs.

Alice had to warn them.

Just as she turned toward the stairs, though, she heard footsteps.

Duane came hurtling down the steps, crying out Holly's name. Behind him came Becca and Ona.

"No," Alice yelled. "Run. She's got a bomb."

Duane froze. Becca careened into him, followed by Ona, nearly falling over the other two. For a while, they stood as still as stone statues, gazing at Holly and Alice. Then Duane, his voice hushed, said, "Holly, how do we stop the bomb?"

"You don't," she said. "Only I know how to stop the bomb…"

Two minutes.

Alice turned back to Holly. "Do you want to die?"

Holly didn't react. She sat immobile in the chair, staring at the photograph of her and her mother. And Alice realized Holly did want to die. This was her Plan B. When she visited Wonderland Books, she'd revealed that she had life insurance. Her one big expense, she'd called it. Alice didn't need the numbers. She could guess the payout would be significant. Significant enough to take care of her mom's medical bills.

She crouched down and touched Holly's hands, which were balled up in her lap.

She said, "You think your mom will thank you for killing yourself and leaving her alone with a big check from the insurance company?"

"She'll be taken care of."

"She'll be broken."

Holly flinched. "You don't know her."

She pulled her hands away from under Alice's touch and reached out for the photograph. She pulled it to her, clutching it to her chest.

One minute.

Holly doubled over the photograph, sobbing. The red scarf slipped loose and spilled onto the floor. As it coiled into a pile at Alice's feet, a memory flashed across her mind. Holly's mom in the bookstore wearing her striking outfit. The Daphne Du Maurier book she'd picked out.

Red and black.

Thirty seconds.

She studied the metal box. Red wire. Blue wire. Green wire. And there: red wire twisted around a black one. It was a hunch, no more—but a hunch that might save their lives.

Twenty seconds.

She reached across the table and grasped the two coiled wires—the red and the black—and she hesitated. If she was wrong...

Ten seconds.

Her throat constricted. She could no longer breathe.

She pulled. The wires resisted her tug, then popped out of their socket.

She gasped.

The clock had stopped counting down, paused at 7 seconds.

Alice held the wires in her hand, the only sound in the cellar the hammering of her heart and Holly's soft sobbing.

CHAPTER 32

*a*fternoon light reflected off the thick snow blanketing the Blithedale Woods. The heater in Ona's pickup pumped hot air as they rumbled down the road. Alice sat pressed up against Becca on the passenger's side.

Then Becca pointed. "There it is."

Ona slowed the pickup, and they drifted past the old Victorian mansion. Alice hadn't been back since the night Holly confessed to the murders in the cellar. The house looked peaceful, its roof adorned with snow. The yard, which had been used for parking during the haunted house show, was a field of white. A chain hung across the entry. A sign said, "Private property: stay out." Another by the side of the road revealed that MacDonald Realty had sold the property.

"So Peyton finally sold the place," Alice said.

"I wonder who bought it," Ona said.

Becca had the answer. "Mayor MacDonald told me she sold to a company that runs assisted living facilities. It seems ironic, doesn't it? Holly's mom may end up living in the house her daughter was going to blow up."

Alice knew none of them actually thought it was ironic. Tragic, yes. But not ironic.

Becca mentioned that the refurbishment of the old Victorian would begin in spring. The house vanished from view as they drove on. The three of them lapsed into silence. The house might look peaceful, but it carried enough bad memories to put a damper on their mood. Alice was glad the new owners would transform it and make it serve a new purpose.

Holly was in prison for murder. Duane, for concealing the truth, had gotten a shorter sentence for accessory and obstructing justice. No mysteries remained unsolved. Except one, maybe. How Chief Jimbo could possibly claim to have played such a key role in solving the case. He was telling everyone that arresting Becca and keeping her locked up had been part of his brilliant plan.

"The killer got sloppy," he'd explained. "She thought she was safe, because the police—me—insisted Becca had done it. But it was all part of my master plan to smoke out the murderer."

Alice didn't contradict him. She was used to Chief Jimbo by now. Besides, he'd let them off the hook for breaking out of jail.

Ona sighed, bringing Alice back to the present moment.

"Thank God Halloween is over…" Ona said and reached for the radio dial and turned it on.

A bluegrass band was playing a spirited rendition of "Rudolph the Red-Nosed Reindeer." It took a moment for Alice to realize they were listening to the Pointed Firs.

"This is Althea and her band," she said.

Ona grinned. "Didn't you hear? Their holiday single is a hit."

Becca stomped a foot in time to the music. Ona joined in with Althea's voice, and soon the three of them were singing along at the tops of their voices. There was nothing subtle about the performance. And maybe it wasn't pretty. But it was pure joy. Alice belted the song, laughing and clapping when they came to the end.

"Impeccable timing," Ona said, and turned the pickup into the parking lot by the Woodlander Bar.

Alice and Becca got out of the pickup on the passenger side. Ona got out, too, and then joined them. The three of them admired the changes.

A patio cover had been erected over the serving area. The roof was laden with snow, but sheltered beneath it sat the usual tables. In their midst stood the Pointed Firs, Althea's band, playing a jaunty bluegrass tune. Another Christmas classic: "O' Come All Ye Faithful." Patio heaters suspended from the roof kept the guests warm. A crowd stood by the door to Thor's tiny house, and Alice spotted Mayor MacDonald and Todd Townsend sipping from mugs of steaming mulled wine.

But the biggest change was that Thor's tiny house was no longer alone. Another tiny house stood across from it — on the other side of the area with the tables. It had a sign out front that said:

UNDER THE GREENWOOD TREE

As Alice admired Ona's handiwork, Edie emerged from within, carrying a tray with plates of food. She smiled when she saw Alice.

"I'm going to take a look," Alice told Ona and Becca, and headed over to the tiny house.

As soon as she got inside, she met a long counter, behind which was the kitchen. Dylan moved behind a gas stove, working on the food. Fleur stood behind the counter.

"Alice," she said with a big smile. "Hungry?"

Alice looked at Dylan's menu of the day, detailed on a

large chalkboard. If she thought she wasn't hungry before, she definitely was after seeing what the restaurant was offering: French beef stew, Thanksgiving-style turkey sandwiches, and a soup du jour. Quality comfort food.

Ona and Becca joined her, stomping their boots at the entrance to get the snow off.

Dylan left the kitchen and came to the counter to say hello.

"Business is already good," he said. "Thanks to you all."

"Thanks to the Blithedale Fund," Alice said.

After a local hearing, a majority of citizens voted to provide a start-up loan for Dylan's restaurant. But as usual, townies had done more than provide a loan. Ona had donated a tiny house, tailor-making one to accommodate a kitchen, while Alice and Becca had helped promote the restaurant. Thor's suggestion that Dylan open his restaurant next to his bar was a stroke of genius—now people went for a drink at the Woodlander and stayed for dinner at the Greenwood Tree, or went for dinner and ordered drinks from next door. Both businesses would thrive.

Alice, Becca, and Ona ordered food. Then got drinks from Thor's bar. Once they got comfy under a heater, they sipped their mulled wine and listened to the Pointed Firs play holiday tunes.

It was more than mulled wine that warmed Alice's insides. She loved her friends and this cozy town in the woods. Edie and Fleur, now employed at Dylan's restaurant, were learning the important lesson she herself had, at first, struggled with: friendship and love don't just depend on lending a hand; they also depend on asking for help when you need it. If Holly had learned that lesson, she might've discovered that Blithedale was the kind of place where people were happy to lift you out of whatever rut you were in.

"Ladies," she said, raising her mug. "Here's to friends looking out for each other."

Ona raised her mug. Becca did, too.

Ona said, "And to the ghosts of Halloween past."

"With emphasis on *past*," Becca said. "No more ghosts, please."

Ona chuckled. "How about reindeer, candy canes, and mistletoe?"

"And mulled wine," Alice added. "Lots of mulled wine."

They clinked mugs and drank. They listened to the music. Like the effect of the mulled wine, Alice felt the holiday spirit warm her—right down to her bones.

She made a prediction: This was going to be a cozy Christmas. The absolute coziest.

* * *

Thank you so much for visiting Blithedale. Join Alice and her friends for another cozy mystery in book 3:

A Christmas to Die For

Oh, and want a FREE short story? Sign up for my newsletter updates on new books and I'll send the free story to you by email:

https://mpblackbooks.com/newsletter/

Finally, if you enjoyed this book, please take a moment to leave a review online. It makes it easier for other readers to find the book. Thanks so much!

Turn the page to read chapter 1 of *A Christmas to Die For* (Book 4)...

A CHRISTMAS TO DIE FOR
EXCERPT

*O*nderland Books—which looked like a miniature log-cabin—measured about 400 square feet, and so it was a tight squeeze to host so many people for the Clyde Digby book reading. The author himself sat on a tall stool at the opposite end from the small counter, right under a sprig of mistletoe.

From behind the counter, Alice Hartford worried. She worried that the audience, most of them standing and pressed against each other or a bookshelf, were uncomfortable. She worried the bestselling Digby was unhappy reading to such a small audience. And looking at her watch, she worried the event would run out of time and it would delay the next reading—the children's story hour with Santa Claus.

"Calm down," her friend Ona Rodriguez said. The eye-patch she wore over one eye glittered with rhinestones. "Everyone's loving this. Clyde Digby's great. And there's plenty of time before the story hour for the kids starts."

"But no sign of Santa yet."

"There's still time. Relax. Focus on Digby's reading instead—he's amazing."

Alice let out a long sigh. Maybe Ona was right. She ought to enjoy this. The bookstore looked festive, with ornaments hanging from bookshelves and from the log-cabin beams above. A bonsai tree, cut and decorated like a miniature Christmas tree, stood on her counter. And near the door, a mannequin in a Santa costume welcomed visitors. It had a bag of treats around its neck and a small sign that said, "Ho! Ho! Ho! Grab a candy cane!"

She pushed aside the dozen to-do's fluttering around in her head and focused on Clyde Digby.

The fifty-ish author—a balding, cardigan-wearing man with a giant, graying beard—was reading from his latest book, a novella called "The Mistletoe Scandal." Alice had a stack of the thin paperbacks in her bookstore, including on the counter. Ahead of the reading, she'd sold more copies of this one book than any other this year.

The cover was enticing: It showed a hunky, bare-chested guy kissing a woman on her neck under a sprig of mistletoe. The woman, head thrown back, was in a state of ecstasy.

The cover had another thing in its favor: A sticker announced the author would donate his proceeds from book sales to a charity.

From his perch on the stool, Digby read:

"He gestured at something above her head.
  'Mistletoe again,' he said.
  'Miles, this time...'
  'Yes?'
  'Kiss me.'
  And he did. He kissed her with an intensity that she'd longed for—that she now understood she needed more than anything—and her body burned with what felt like a lifetime of pent-up passion."

The audience held its breath. As Digby continued his reading, the bookstore was so silent Alice could hear the crunch of boots on the snow outside.

Convincing Digby to do a reading at Blithedale's tiny bookstore had been a major coup. He was a bestselling romance author with a home in the Blithedale Woods (and another in Costa Rica, plus an apartment in New York City). For most of his career, he'd published under pseudonyms—Jessica Spence, Leigh Lowry, Madeleine Darcy—but in recent years, he'd switched to his own name. His readers didn't mind; his sales had only increased. Alice hadn't read his novels, which ranged from sweet contemporary to spicy Regency romances, but Ona had.

A stack of Ona's Clyde Digby paperbacks, including a few under pseudonyms, sat on the counter. She'd taken a break from work at her hotel—the Pemberley Inn—hoping Digby would sign them all.

Digby reached the end of his reading and the audience let out a collective sigh. Then people clapped. The first eager fans rushed forward to get their books signed. Shoes shuffled, heavy winter overcoats rustled, and chatter filled Wonderland Books.

"Wow," Ona said.

"As good as you'd expected?" Alice asked.

"Better. I'm going to get in line."

Ona grabbed her stack of books and headed for the throng of people gathered at the other end near Digby.

Meanwhile, Alice got busy helping customers. A woman from out of town bought a stack of books, including Digby's novella and *A Christmas Carol* by Charles Dickens. She spoke of getting into the Christmas spirit, and as Alice rang up her purchases, she told the customer about the Blithedale Christmas Fair.

"I saw an ad for it online," the woman said. "Sounds wonderful. Is it a tradition?"

Alice nodded. "But I'm told it was modest in past years. We've expanded it a lot. We're going to have a parade with horse carriages, and if you walk a little way down Main Street, you'll see the fairgrounds with rows and rows of stalls. Vendors are selling crafts and clothes and food."

"Oh, I'll have to check it out. And I'll come back with my husband and kids, too." She took her bag of books from Alice. "I came for Digby's reading and didn't know what to expect. I'm surprised at how quaint this town is. Blithedale has a shady reputation, doesn't it? I mean, there's been several murders."

Another customer in line spoke up. He said, "Yeah, I read about the murders, too. And I actually came to town years ago and visited the bookstore—" He looked around. "—but it looked different back then. And the owner was so rude, I left."

"His name is Bunce," Alice muttered.

"Is he your boss?"

"He's not my boss," Alice said emphatically, annoyed that he'd assume Bunce—Bunce, of all people—was her boss. Then, aware that she'd snapped at the customer, she softened her tone. "This is my business. This is my bookstore. The old Blithedale Books is gone."

In fact, Blithedale Books was originally owned by Alice's mom. But when her mom got cancer, she sold to Bunce, and 9-year-old Alice and her mom moved from Blithedale. When Alice returned earlier this year—20 years after she'd left, 20 years after her mom had died—she discovered a run-down Blithedale Books, neglected by a bitter, mean old Bunce. Eventually, bulldozers tore down the old bookstore and Alice established a new one, Wonderland Books.

She took a deep breath and let it out. The old bookstore

and Bunce were both gone. Soon, people would forget about the cantankerous bookseller and his shabby store. Time would obscure the past. She hoped they would forget about the recent murders, too, and instead think of Blithedale as the best place in the world to celebrate Christmas.

Alice and her friends, Ona and Becca, had drawn on their own business reserves to invest in this year's Christmas Fair. Plus, the Blithedale Future Fund—a community investment fund run by the three of them to revitalize businesses in town—had contributed a lot to the budget. Everyone was counting on the Christmas fair being a success.

And if it isn't...? If no one shows up...?

Everyone was counting on the event to draw big crowds and increase revenue for the town.

As part of Blithedale's ongoing efforts to revitalize, Mayor Townsend had invested heavily in this year's fair. A demolition contractor had torn down an abandoned office building to make space for the fairgrounds. An event production company had been contracted to develop holiday parade floats. They also provided horse carriages and horses to pull the floats, stalls, porta-potties, and sound systems— plus a generator to run it all.

To pay for everything, the Blithedale Municipality had taken a short-term loan from the Tilbury Savings and Loans Bank. It would need to be repaid at the beginning of next year. If the fair failed, the town—heavily indebted—would face serious financial problems. And by extension, so would local businesses like her bookstore. They were all betting a lot on this event.

As another customer brought a pile of books to the counter, she pushed the negative thoughts aside. People were buying books. And she told each out-of-towner about the fair, hoping they'd come back or tell their friends. Ideally both.

We're all doing what we can.

As the romance fans shuffled out, parents with children wandered into Wonderland Books. Alice checked her watch again. The organizers of the fair had assigned a Santa Claus to come for the story hour. He should've arrived by now.

She grabbed her phone and dialed the number for Ben Ridgeway, who was involved in staffing the fair. Resting her phone under her cheek, so she could have her hands free, she gift wrapped books for a customer: hardbound editions of *The Adventure of the Blue Carbuncle* by Arthur Conan Doyle and *Hercule Poirot's Christmas* by Agatha Christie.

"Hi, Ben—the Santa Claus I ordered, well, he's not here…"

Ben asked her to hold while he checked.

"Alice, sorry about this. Vickers, who's in charge of the Santa contest and the Santas, he says the guy should arrive any moment now."

She hung up and tended to the next customer, who was buying more Clyde Digby books. Then Ona returned with her pile of signed books, a big grin on her face.

"It's like Christmas came early," she said. "Who doesn't love a pile of books?"

A man in a Santa costume shambled into the bookstore, and Alice thought, *Finally, now we can get the kids' story hour started.*

But when he turned toward her and scowled, she froze. Despite the fake Santa beard, she recognized his pasty face at once. Her heart did a backflip.

"Bunce?"

"Books," he grumbled, looking around at the bookstore with disdain. "I hate books."

Want more? Join Alice and her friends in the next book: *A Christmas to Die For*

MORE BY M.P. BLACK

ABOUT THE AUTHOR

M.P. Black writes fun cozies with an emphasis on food, books, and travel — and, of course, a good old murder mystery.

In addition to writing and publishing his own books, he helps others fulfill their author dreams too.

M.P. Black has lived in many places, including Austria, Costa Rica, and the United Kingdom. Today, he lives in Copenhagen, Denmark, with his family.

Join M.P. Black's free newsletter for updates on books and special deals:

https://mpblackbooks.com/newsletter/

Printed in Great Britain
by Amazon